The Bride of Lilly Pilly Creek
Abbie L. Martin

Book 2 - A Lilly Pilly Creek Ghost Mystery

THE BRIDE OF LILLY PILLY CREEK

Imprint: Abbie Allen Publishing
Cover art by Abbie Allen

For information address Abbie L. Martin abbielmartinauthor@gmail.com

ISBN: 978-0-6457139-5-4
Abbie L. Martin paperback edition / August 2023
Abbie L. Martin books are published by Abbie Allen Publishing

CHAPTER 1

Jones woke to the sound of haunting singing. Fear clutched her heart and in her sleepiness she was confused. She was supposed to be home alone. Slowly, she dared open her eyes. At the foot of her bed, a ghostly figure loomed over her. With long auburn hair and a bright red ball gown, the ghost was grinning.

"Autumn! What are you doing here?"

Jones smiled at her sister, happy to see her. No matter how often she saw Autumn's translucent form, Jones was always somewhat surprised that her sister was truly back from the dead.

"I wanted to see how far I could travel on my own!" Autumn twirled and then stood, palms up, presenting herself to Jones.

"Are you ok?" Jones asked, eyes widening with worry. She had snapped out of her sleepy state and remembered Autumn didn't usually travel far on her own, without Jones. The sisters hadn't yet worked out exactly how Autumn's energy functioned.

"We need to get you back to the Memory Bank." Jones slid across the bed and swung her legs over the side.

"I'm fine, Jones," said Autumn. "I feel great!" She walked to the window and elegantly propped herself up on the windowsill. "I mean, it's taken a bit out of me, but I'm fine."

"Autumn! You really shouldn't do things like this," said Jones. She had stood up and was rifling through her wardrobe, trying to find an outfit for the unusually wet November weather she could see beyond Autumn.

This morning Jones grabbed a long dusty pink cardigan, some navy corduroy trousers, and a white t-shirt with Mary Poppins song lyrics across the front *"Winds in the east, mist coming in. Like somethin' is brewin' and 'bout to begin. Can't put me finger on what lies in store, but I feel what's to happen all happened before."* As she bent to pull a pair of tan loafers out from under her bed she glanced at Autumn.

"Do you have enough energy to stop at Sybil's on the way?"

"Of course I do," said Autumn, before hesitating. "Where is she parked at the moment?"

"I'm pretty sure I saw her near the pub last night," said Jones. "That's on the way. Do you think you'll be ok?"

"Yes, I'll be with *you*, and we know that always helps." The sisters paused for a moment to smile at each other. Over the last few months, they had become the closest they'd ever been, even more so than when they were children. It was ironic that their closeness had come because, for a reason yet unknown to them, Autumn had returned to earth as a ghost after her death. After her murder.

Only weeks ago, the sisters had worked together, using Autumn's ghostly talents, to discover that Autumn's ex-boyfriend Jamie had pushed her down a spiral staircase in a fit of rage. The same spiral staircase that was a feature of the family business, The Memory Bank.

As Jones got dressed she reflected on how proud she was to now be custodian of The Memory Bank. A bookshop come stationery store come gift shop, The Memory Bank had been in the family for decades. Up until Autumn's death, Jones hadn't even considered running the business. Now she found she was enjoying the daily interaction with customers, ordering stock, and in particular the lockboxes, unique to The Memory Bank which meant it stood out from every other shop in the Adelaide Hills.

"Is Atlas in today?" asked Autumn, following Jones to the kitchen.

"Yes," said Jones. "He's coming in mid-morning so I can go and visit Iris."

"Oh, is her lockbox almost finished?" Whilst Jones took her handbag and made sure it contained everything she needed, Autumn was slowly rising and falling on repeat, her head touching the ceiling before she floated back down to the floor.

"Yes," said Jones. "I'm going to meet with Iris today just to check everything off and ensure I've collected everyone's items."

"This time capsule is such a great idea!" said Autumn. "Instead of just storing your own memories in one of our lockboxes, it's genius to ask others to share their memories of you, so they can be opened later. How did Iris get the idea?"

"I'm not sure," said Jones. "She said she wanted to do something different for her wedding. It really is clever." Jones slung her handbag over her shoulder. "Ready?"

"As ready as I'll ever be!"

As usual, Autumn moved quickly ahead, showing off by travelling directly through walls instead of the doorways that Jones had to use. Even now Jones still found the whole thing bizarre, to watch her sister disappear from one room to the next.

Jones grabbed a heavy rain jacket that was hanging on a hat stand, before opening the front door. There she found Autumn standing on a fence post, waiting for her.

"You've really got a sense of the dramatic, haven't you," said Jones, laughing at her sister.

"Why stand on the ground when I can stand anywhere I like!" With that, Autumn pushed herself off and managed a mid-air somersault, her red ballgown ballooning, before slowly coming back to earth. The rain didn't affect Autumn as it did Jones, who pulled her jacket hood over her head and did her best to hide her face from the rain.

Jones regularly walked instead of driving to The Memory Bank, although this morning she wondered if she had made the right decision as the rain came down.

"Seriously," said Jones. "I can't believe how wet it's been for November. This is unusual, right?"

"That's what I heard the farmers saying outside the post office the other day," said Autumn.

"When were you at the post office?" Jones had her hands shoved into her jacket, very much looking forward to a cup of Sybil's hot coffee.

"When you were helping Mr Phelps with his lockbox the other day. He was taking forever and I was bored, so I thought I'd start my experiment to see how far I can go by myself."

"You're running an experiment?" Jones raised her eyebrows.

"Well, it seems ridiculous to think that as a ghost I could only hang around The Memory Bank unless I'm with you," said Autumn. "How helpful is that going to be for The Eldershaw Sisters Detective

Agency?"

Jones laughed. It was a little inside joke the sisters had. After working together to solve the mystery of Autumn's murder, they imagined starting their own detective agency. The pair were a great team, and with Autumn's ability to move in places others couldn't, it meant they had often found themselves one step ahead of the police. Unfortunately, the fact that Autumn was a ghost also made it impossible for them to start a real detective agency together. But they pretended all the same.

"Well, that is true," said Jones. "Just don't push yourself too hard. We don't know what happens if you lose all your energy. I just couldn't bare it...." Jones couldn't bring herself to finish that sentence. She had already lost her sister once. The miracle of Autumn's return meant Jones had a second chance to spend time with her, and get to know her better. The thought of losing her again was something Jones did her best to avoid.

"Jones!" They heard Sybil calling out loudly before they were even close to the coffee van. "Do you want a toasted sandwich?"

A hot snack to start her day sounded ideal. "Yes please!" Jones called back. Through the rain she watched Sybil pop something into a sandwich press before turning to the coffee machine. Sybil knew Jones's regular order, a strong flat white with full cream milk. Jones had tasted many a flat white during her time as a journalist in the city, but Sybil's coffee beat everything she had ever tried in Adelaide.

By the time Jones had managed to push her way through the rain and up to Sybil, her steaming floral takeaway cup of coffee was sitting ready for her, and Sybil was just putting the toasted sandwich into a paper bag. On the back counter, Frank the ginger cat was curled up, sound asleep.

"I thought you wouldn't want to stand around too long in this rain and wait for it to cook," said Sybil, explaining why she had yelled down the street instead of waiting for Jones to arrive.

"You read my mind, Sybil," said Jones. "I mean, what on earth is this weather anyway?"

"It's ridiculous!" said Sybil. "But I am doing a bit of a roaring trade in drive-through coffees."

"Drive-through?" Jones was a little confused. Sybil's coffee van was nothing like a McDonald's. It was a cute, vintage caravan, painted an eye-catching mauve and cream, with a servery window, and a timber sign that simply said 'Sybil's Coffee'.

"I've had people ringing in orders all morning," Sybil explained. "They come past, jump out their car, grab it and go."

"I love that idea!" said Jones. "I can see I'm going to take advantage of this new service."

"Go for it," said Sybil. "And are you nearly finished with your project for Iris and Drew? The wedding is just under two weeks away, isn't it?"

"It sure is," said Jones. Sybil knew everything about the town of Lilly Pilly Creek, so it wasn't surprising that she was keeping tabs on Jones and the development of the memory box she was creating. "I'm meeting Iris today for a few last-minute things."

"Sounds lovely. What a wonderful idea it is." Sybil smiled and a mobile phone trilled behind her. "Here we go again!'

Jones waved, left Sybil to her takeaway order, and continued her wet trek to The Memory Bank.

CHAPTER 2

One of Jones's favourite things was pulling out her heavy metal key and placing it in the lock of The Memory Bank's large, wooden front door. The twist and clunk as it unlocked, before pushing the door open with her hip, was a joy she was sure she would never get over. Next, since a new security system had been recently installed as a result of a rather dramatic break-in, Jones walked to the keypad and entered the code. With a beep, it was turned off.

Usually, Autumn was inside waiting for Jones. But today Autumn stood by her, waiting after surprisingly entering through the doorway rather than the door itself.

"Do it," whispered Autumn.

Jones knew what Autumn was referring to. She flipped the master light switch and together they slowly walked into the main room of the Bank. Bare bulbs lit up immediately, but it was the main event that Jones and Autumn waited for. Above them, in the very centre of the room, they watched as the giant candelabra flickered to life. It was an impressive sight, and no matter how many times she saw it, Jones was always a little in awe.

After a moment's pause, it was back to business. Placing her handbag behind the curved counter, brass letters spelling out 'The Memory Bank' which glowed under the light of the candelabra, Jones took a final sip of her coffee before tossing the cup into their recycling bin. She took a box of matches, and as she did each morning, made her way around The Memory Bank, lighting candles throughout the room.

She loved the atmosphere it gave the shop area, and it didn't hurt that a selection of candles was available for sale, amongst the stationery, books, and other gifts that were always ready for purchase on the wooden tables and shelves.

"So, you've collected nearly everyone's bits and pieces to go into Drew and Iris's Memory Box," said Autumn. "How are the interviews going?"

"All finished!" said Jones. "Well, the interviewing part. Now I have to pull everything together and turn it into a readable story. That's going to be quite a task."

"Yes, it's not long until the wedding!"

"I have to get cracking if I'm going to have the memory book printed in time for the big day."

"Are you going to make it?" Autumn looked genuinely concerned.

"Absolutely! I'm a journalist remember? I'm used to working to tight deadlines. This will be a walk in the park." Despite her confident declaration, Jones had to admit she was feeling a little anxious about the project. Yes, she was a journalist by trade, but she hadn't worked as a journalist since her sister's death almost five months ago. Jones was a little worried she may be out of practice and was desperately hoping the riding a bike theory was true.

This memory box project was different to the usual lockboxes they dealt with in The Memory Bank. Lockboxes were one of the most popular services they offered. As The Memory Bank was housed in an old bank, when her Grandparents bought the building it came with the original safety deposit boxes. It was Jones and Autumn's Grandmother who came up with the brilliant idea of using them to store her family history items. When word got around, people approached their Grandmother, asking if they could store their memories in the lockboxes too. Thus, The Memory Bank was born!

Jones looked up at the large clock she had recently put on the wall. It echoed the size and shape of the clock on the tower at the top of the building. Unfortunately, the tower clock hadn't worked for many years, but the new wall clock showed Jones it was nearly time to open up for the first customers. Since the grand reopening, the first day an absolute triumph, they'd had a steady stream of customers, both new and regulars. Many were adding things to their lockboxes, but The Memory Bank had become a place for people to buy gifts, replenish their stationery, or pick up a book connected to the local area. The Memory Bank had always been an establishment in Lilly Pilly Creek, but with Jones's personal touch, helped by the ghostly support of Autumn, the family business had once again been reinvigorated and was a haven for many of the visitors.

"I still think two things are missing from The Memory Bank." Jones unlocked the front door but kept it closed to keep the wind and wet at bay.

"Oh yes," said Autumn, perched up on top of the counter, legs crossed. It was a familiar location for her. "What would those be?"

"A nice garden area for people to sit in," Jones said, looking towards the outside area. Even though it was raining, it was a light-filled area that currently consisted of gravel, weeds and a few dying plants in pots. "And coffee!"

"You want to become a barista now?" Autumn raised her eyebrows.

"No!" Jones laughed. "Not at all! Couldn't think of anything worse. But Sybil's drive-through comment has sparked something. I'm not sure what the answer is, but imagine if people could get Sybil's coffee *inside* The Memory Bank?"

"Like literally inside?" asked Autumn. The vision of Sybil's coffee van inside on the floor of The Memory Bank was both a ludicrous and glorious sight.

"I'm not sure yet," said Jones. "I have an inkling of an idea forming, but I just can't pin it down."

"Well, whilst you ponder that, you'd better serve your first customer."

Jones started, surprised to see that a woman and three young children had walked into the store. She smiled, winked at Autumn, and made her way over to the group, who were looking at a selection of colourful notebooks on a stand just near the entrance.

It was ten thirty when Atlas arrived. He came lugging a laptop bag and two cups of coffee. He always knew Jones would welcome a second cup at this time of the morning. His glasses were covered in rain drops and it was clear he had struggled to get the door open.

"Atlas! Let me help!" said Jones. She rushed over, grabbed both coffees and offered to take his bag also.

"I'm ok," said Atlas, pulling his glasses off. "I just need a tissue to wipe these. What is it with this weather?"

"Tell me about it," said Jones. "It's November. I bet this is one of the wettest on record."

Jones placed the coffee on the counter, before moving behind and pulling out a tissue box.

"That's better!" said Atlas, popping his freshly wiped glasses back on.

"Thanks so much for coming in today Atlas," said Jones. "I know it isn't your usual day."

"Not a problem," said Atlas. "Just as long as you're happy for me to work on my laptop when there's a lull." Atlas plonked his laptop bag down and began unzipping.

"Of course!" said Jones.

Atlas had been an integral part of Jones being able to reopen The Memory Bank. He had worked with her side-by-side, assisting with the renovations, and, most importantly, digitising all the old ledgers so the records were now on the computer. It was Atlas's work with the ledgers that had been one of the reasons they were able to discover who had killed Autumn, along with a few other secrets along the way. Jones would be forever grateful for everything Atlas had done. Atlas in turn was fiercely loyal to Jones and The Memory Bank and was always happy to help when he could. He had some regular shifts each week, but Jones found herself calling on him more often in recent weeks, whilst she travelled around the Adelaide Hills collecting memories for Iris Wainwright's memory box.

"I shouldn't be too long," said Jones. "I just have to meet Iris at her dress fitting. I think she was given some things from family members over the weekend to put in her memory box."

"So it's nearly finished?" Atlas's eyes were wide. He had heard about this project every step of the way and knew what a big deal this was.

"So close!" said Jones. "This next week I'm going to be busy typing up the interviews, ready to print."

"It's such a brilliant idea," said Atlas, smiling at Jones before turning to his laptop.

"Well, I'll leave you to it!" said Jones.

Atlas waved her away, telling her everything was fine. Jones knew The Memory Bank was in safe hands.

"Shall we depart?" said Autumn, gliding up to Jones and sliding her gossamer arm into Jones's elbow.

"Shhh!" said Jones. "But yes."

"You always tell me to be quiet, but you're the only one who can hear me!" Autumn said this deliberately loudly, just to shock her sister. Jones shook her head but didn't respond. She didn't want Atlas asking who she was talking to.

Jones grabbed her handbag and together they left The Memory Bank.

CHAPTER 3

"How far are we going?" asked Autumn. Instead of heading past Hugo's wine bar, Jones was taking them across the road into another section of Lilly Pilly Creek.

"I believe the Tailor is behind Wren's office," said Jones.

"Tailor? For a dress fitting? Don't you mean dressmaker?" Autumn looked bemused.

"I have no idea, Autumn," said Jones. "I'm not an expert in altering dresses. A tailor alters suits, I guess they can alter dresses too." The look on Autumn's face showed she wasn't convinced, but she glided alongside Jones anyway, enjoying another trip outside The Memory Bank.

They walked past Wren's office and peered through the windows, but her desk was empty. Immediately next door was their destination.

'Manowski Tailors' could just be seen printed in very faded white text on the brick wall of the building. Jones took hold of the chrome handle that was positioned diagonally across the glass door and pushed. With a long creak, accompanied by the dinging of a bell, it opened into a dark room. On either side of them were stands holding bolts of fabric. It was like a maze and Jones had no idea which direction she should turn. Luckily, she had a ghost at her disposal and before long Autumn had found where Iris was.

"They're in the back room," said Autumn. "It's light and bright in there!"

"Hello!" Jones called out as she made her way, not wanting to startle anyone, especially a bride at her final dress fitting.

"Is that you Jones?" A female's voice was heard from beyond. "We're back here!"

Jones made her way through the fabric racks, following Autumn's lead to a doorway, the rooms separated by a heavy brocade curtain.

"Hello?" Jones said again, before pushing her way through.

Jones walked in, confused, as this room also appeared empty. Autumn was right, it was much lighter and brighter. It was quite lovely. Everything was white and clean. On one side was a long navy velvet couch, sitting underneath a large window, covered with sheer curtains. In the middle of the room was a round dais where, Jones guessed, the customer would stand to have their clothes pinned. Opposite the navy couch on the other side of the room, was a sleek wooden desk, holding the tools of the tailor's trade. Finally, there were two curtained fitting rooms.

"I'm in here Jones," said Iris. "Just getting my dress on. I'll be out in a minute! Grab a seat."

Jones went over to the velvet couch whilst Autumn floated away through a wall, no doubt taking a look around. Jones wondered where the tailor was. She sat quietly, listening to the rustle of Iris's dress behind the curtain, looking at the walls that were adorned with vintage fashion plates; women in gorgeous gowns and men in tuxedos and three-piece suits.

"He's coming," said Autumn whizzing back into the room. A moment later a small door at the side of the room opened, and in walked a short man, with a black moustache, wearing a smart, formal grey suit, and his black hair slicked down against his head.

"Hi," said Jones.

The man's eyes darted towards her. He frowned, nodded, and went and sat behind his desk.

'Well,' thought Jones. 'I guess you're not a conversationalist.'

"Mr Manowski?" called Iris. "Are you ready for me?"

"Yes Miss Wainwright," he responded, clasping his hands on the desk in front of him.

Autumn positioned herself by the dais, and Jones found herself inching forward on the couch.

The dressing room curtains parted and out walked a stunning woman in a simple, yet gorgeous bridal gown.

"Wow!" said Autumn. Jones's eyes flicked at her in warning, but then said in an equal amount of awe "Oh Iris, you look gorgeous."

The blonde bride beamed at Jones. "Do you really think so?"

"Absolutely!" Jones stood, taking in the sweetheart neckline, sheer lace over the shoulders, and the skirt's fabric which pooled gently at her feet.

"I'm not done up or anything," Iris said. "But when it's on properly and taken in a bit, I think I might be able to pull it off."

"Drew is going to love it!" said Jones.

"If you please, Miss Wainwright," said Mr Manowski, indicating for Iris to take her position on the dais.

Stepping up, Iris turned to face Jones so they could talk.

"Thank you so much for coming to me today," said Iris. "I was struggling to find a time to catch up."

"Not a problem at all," said Jones. "It's not far from The Memory Bank."

"It's just, I've been sick for the last week, and it has thrown out my timeline."

"Sick?" asked Jones. "Are you ok now?" Jones peered at Iris and did notice darkness under her eyes and slightly sallow skin.

"Yes, I finally seem to be picking up," said Iris. "A tummy bug or something. It's taken quite a bit to get out of bed and out of the house. But today is a good day. I even managed to eat a little at lunch."

Although Iris seemed quite positive, Jones couldn't help but feel concerned for her new friend. Especially since, in preparation for her interviews over the past few weeks, Iris had shared with Jones that as a teenager she had had leukaemia, and many people had brought up her remission when they spoke with Jones. No doubt this thought had crossed Iris's mind too, and it certainly wasn't Jones's place to mention it.

Mr Manowski worked silently, pulling pins from his pocket, marking the dress with a piece of pink chalk, and taking the tape measure from his neck to check his work.

"Where did you go for lunch?" Jones asked.

"Harris cooked! We went to the winery where he works, with Drew's family. Sort of a pre-wedding catch-up. It was quite busy, but Harris did a great job. He is very good in the kitchen."

"Who's Harris again?" Autumn whispered. She had come to take a seat next to Jones.

"Drew's brother," Jones whispered under her breath.

"Sorry?" Iris said, thinking Jones was speaking to her.

"Lovely," said Jones. "I said that sounds lovely. And that's the same winery where you're having the wedding?"

"Yes!" Iris smiled. "Casa Galati. The Galati family run it. Amazing wine. We're so lucky. They don't often have weddings but Harris said Tara insisted."

"Tara?" asked Jones.

"Tara Galati," said Iris, and Jones was sure she saw Iris's mouth tighten slightly. "Tara is the head winemaker now. She took over from her father a few years ago."

"Ah yes, I think she was a few years ahead of me in school," said Jones. Jones could picture her. A very tall, striking girl with a big personality. Never someone Jones had had much to do with, but she got the impression it wasn't hard for Tara to rub people the wrong way. "So, Harris isn't joining Drew on the family farm?"

"No," said Iris. "Not his thing. Drew just loves the farm, but Harris is different. He seems very happy at the winery. He's travelled all over, working in different kitchens, so he finally gets to run his own. Drew and I don't complain. We get to eat there a lot!"

"Sounds like a dream!" Jones smiled and then frowned. Iris suddenly appeared a little pale and brought her hand to her forehead.

"Mr Manowski," said Iris. "Are we almost done? I'm just feeling a little wonky."

"One more pin," said Mr Manowski, pausing as he placed the final pin at the back of the dress. "And we are done! You may get down."

Iris smiled, and quickly made her way into the changing room.

"Are you ok Iris?" Jones called out. "Can I help?"

But Iris didn't reply. Jones looked worriedly at Autumn. She almost asked Autumn to go in and check but knew that was probably taking things a little too far.

"Iris?"

Suddenly, the dressing room curtains parted and Iris, still in her wedding dress, fell backwards and landed heavily on the floor.

CHAPTER 4

"Iris!" Jones jumped up and ran to the woman laying on the floor. Her eyes were closed, hair and dress splayed around her like Anne Shirley portraying the Lady of Shalott.

"Miss Wainwright!" cried Mr Manowski. It was the first time any sign of emotion had appeared on the man's face.

Jones shook Iris's shoulders gently but she didn't move. "Mr Manowski, call an ambulance, please."

"Right away," he said, picking up the handle of a vintage telephone and dialling triple zero.

"An ambulance, a woman has collapsed," said Mr Manowski into the phone. After providing the address he began calling out instructions to Jones as they were conveyed to him. "Roll her on her side and check her airways," he said.

Jones felt her heart racing. Was it going to be up to her to save Iris's life?

"Come on Jones," said Autumn. "You can do this."

Jones took a deep breath and then, feeling very awkward pulled Iris's right knee up before sliding around to the other side and gently tipped her to the side. She then shuffled back and opened her mouth, making sure she hadn't swallowed her tongue.

"What next, Mr Manowski?" Jones said, looking to the man on the telephone for help. He spoke to the person on the phone before telling Jones, "Is she breathing? Can you feel her breath?" Jones had no idea how to tell, so she put her hand in front of Iris's mouth. She wasn't sure, so she leaned down, trying to both feel and hear for her breath and was relieved when she registered a slight movement of air.

"Yes," said Jones. "Yes, I think she's breathing, although not very well. How far away is the ambulance?"

Jones registered Autumn sliding out of the room. She hoped Autumn would be able to see or hear something.

Jones was feeling a little panicky now. What if the ambulance didn't get here in time? Could they save Iris? And why had she collapsed? Iris had said she was feeling better, and then all of a sudden, she was on the floor.

"They're coming!" Autumn had rushed back into the room. "I could hear them. Very faint but I could hear them. Come on Iris, hold on."

Jones was gripping Iris's hand, talking gently to her, willing her to keep breathing until the ambulance got there. The room was still, with Mr Manowski occasionally mumbling into the telephone. It appeared there was nothing more they could do except wait.

Finally, Jones was able to hear the sirens herself. "Oh thank goodness," she breathed and felt tears of relief pricking her eyes. "Mr Manowski, go out, show them the way." Jones realised she probably sounded bossy, but without a ghost to guide her, Jones didn't know how long it would have taken for her to find the back room. She didn't want the paramedics to waste any time getting to Iris.

Mr Manowski rushed out of the room without hesitation, and although it felt like a lifetime to Jones, soon the curtains were pushed aside and two paramedics in their green uniforms, carrying supplies, were in the room and taking over from Jones. Jones, whose legs were too shaky to walk, scooted herself over to a wall and leant against it, breathing heavily, not taking her eyes off Iris. The paramedics placed an oxygen mask over her face, before listening to her heart and taking her pulse and blood pressure.

"We need to get to the hospital immediately," said one of the women. Turning to Mr Manowski, she asked "Is there an easier way to get the stretcher in here?"

"Certainly," said Mr Manowski. He walked behind the velvet couch and pulled the curtains aside. Clicking a latch, as if by magic the floor-to-ceiling window slid to the side, opening out to the car park behind. A paramedic rushed out and shortly returned with the stretcher.

Very quickly, the experienced paramedics had Iris on the stretcher, loaded up her belongings, and were rolling her out the door.

"I'll try and contact her fiancé," called Jones after the paramedics, and then they were gone.

"Oh my goodness," said Jones, turning in shock to look at Mr Manowski. Jones was surprised to see that he too was now sitting on the floor, leaning up against the dais. The dramatic turn of events had affected him too.

"That poor girl," he said. "I hope she's alright." He turned to Jones. "You will let me know, won't you?"

"Oh course Mr Manowski," said Jones, soothingly. "Of course."

Jones put her hand out to her side and managed to push herself up onto her haunches, before standing. She paused for a moment, checking she was feeling better, and then walked over to Mr Manowski.

Crouching down she asked, "Can I get you anything?"

He looked up at her and furrowed his brow. "Do you think...ah...I mean, would it be appropriate in this circumstance....to have a little nip of vodka? Perhaps?"

Jones heard Autumn laugh and say "I like this man!"

Jones smiled at him. "I think this is the perfect circumstance. Do you have any?"

"No, not here in the shop," he said, shaking his head.

"Shall we go over to Hugo's?" Jones stood up and reached down to help Mr Manowski up.

"Yes," said Mr Manowski. "I can lock up the shop. No other appointments today. Just give me a moment."

"Not a problem," said Jones. "I'll try and call Iris's fiancé."

Jones pulled out her phone and looked through her contact list. She had met with virtually everyone connected to Iris and Drew, including the bride and groom themselves, in pulling together the memory box. She was sure she had his number in her phone and she was right.

"Drew?" she asked when a man answered the phone. "This is Jones Eldershaw. Look, I've just been with Iris at the tailor's, and well, she collapsed."

"Collapsed? What happened? Is she alright?"

"I don't know I'm afraid," said Jones. "The ambulance has been. They're taking her to the Mount Barker Hospital. I think you'd better meet them there."

"Bloody hell! I mean she has been a bit under the weather, but I didn't think it was that bad."

"Drew, she might be ok. Perhaps she was just a bit dehydrated or something. I don't know," said Jones. "But do you have someone to drive you?"

"It's ok, I'm just outside of Hahndorf at the moment looking at some steers. I'm ten minutes away. I'll leave now," he responded. "Thank you, Jones, thank you for calling." And with that, he hung up.

"What did he say?" Autumn asked.

Jones looked around for Mr Manowski but it appeared he was still in the other room locking up.

"He said he's in Hahndorf and he's heading straight there," said Jones. "He was very surprised, of course."

"The poor thing," said Autumn. "I hope she's alright for her wedding."

"Surely!" said Jones. "It's almost two weeks away. It couldn't be that serious?"

"You don't think?" Autumn hesitated. "You don't think perhaps her cancer has come back?"

"I hope not," said Jones, looking down at the floor. "I'm sure Iris is on top of everything, and if she thinks it's just a tummy bug of some sort, then she's probably right."

"Yes, of course," said Autumn. "She's likely just gotten run down with all the wedding preparations."

"Shall we go?" Mr Manowski walked back into the room and held his arm out towards Jones.

She was a little taken aback by the formality, but Mr Manowski was beginning to grow on her. She took his arm, and he lead her out the 'secret' door and towards Hugo's.

CHAPTER 5

As they walked, Mr Manowski having now relinquished Jones's arm so they could both tackle the rain that was again falling, Autumn floated ahead whilst Jones pulled out her phone and hastily rang Atlas.

"Yes, collapsed," she told him.

"Oh my goodness!" said Atlas.

"So, we've decided to go to Hugo's," Jones explained.

"That sounds like a plan," said Atlas. "Do you want me to stay here?"

"I'm happy for you to do what you like," said Jones. "If you need to go, then please just lock up. I'm sure once people find out what's happened, which in this town won't take long, they'll understand why we're closed."

"No worries Jones," said Atlas. "I'll stay a bit longer. I've still got work to do on an assignment anyway. But I will probably need to lock up early afternoon."

"That's fine. I may be feeling ok to come back then anyway," said Jones. "Thanks, Atlas. I seem to be constantly calling in favours."

"Drama does seem to have a way of following you," Atlas chuckled.

"You're not wrong there." Jones hung up just as they arrived at Hugo's.

Mr Manowski pushed the door open and ushered Jones in. She was surprised to find the place packed. Sitting around tables were people dressed like they were hiking the Himalayas. Backpacks were strewn on the floor, and beanies and scarves hung on the back of chairs. Many of them were writing in notebooks, and chatting animatedly over Hugo's lunch menu.

Jones and Mr Manowski made their way to the bar, managing to pull up two stools together between the crowd. Hugo winked at Jones when he saw her, which made her blush, but fortunately, Hugo was too busy serving drinks to notice. Autumn floated throughout the room, eavesdropping on the various conversations.

Eventually, Hugo walked over to Jones and her new companion. "Jones, how can I help you?" He looked at Mr Manowski. "And your friend?"

"Hugo, this is Mr Manowski, the tailor," Jones introduced the men. "We've just had a rather traumatic experience and require a drink.

"Well, that I can do! What can I get you? Your usual, Jones?" Jones smiled and looked down quickly. The fact that he knew her usual pleased her more than she realised. Jones ordered one of her usual gins, and Mr Manowski a neat vodka. "Cold Mr Hugo please, very cold." Hugo nodded with a smile and arranged the drinks.

"Now, can you tell me, what on earth has happened?" Hugo asked, as he placed the drinks in front of them, Jones's garnished with a slice of freeze-dried apple.

"Well, we're not exactly sure," said Jones, leaning forward, indicating that she didn't need the whole wine bar hearing. "I was visiting Iris Wainwright at Mr Manowski's tailor shop," her shoulder indicated the man next to her. "I had to get something from her, so it just made sense to meet her there. And well, she's collapsed and we've just had the ambulance take her to the hospital."

"Really?" Hugo raised his eyebrows, eyes wide.

Jones and Mr Manowski nodded, taking long sips of their drinks.

"What was wrong with her?" Hugo asked.

"We don't know," said Jones. "She said she'd been sick earlier in the week but was feeling much better. Then she went all funny, didn't she Mr Manowski?"

"Yes, yes, all grey, and then plop! She fell on the floor - still wearing her wedding dress!" Mr Manowski explained "Oh, I do hope they don't cut it off her. A tragedy, a tragedy," he said, shaking his head, before taking another sip of his vodka.

"So, these drinks are urgently required," said Jones. "But Hugo, we're keeping you. The bar seems rather busy today?"

"It's all the ghost hunters!"

Jones's head snapped up as he said this, and she felt Autumn whiz next to her.

"Ghost hunters?" Jones asked, feeling her throat catch, almost unable to get the words out.

"Yep," said Hugo, flipping his tea towel over his shoulder and rolling his eyes a touch. "Ghost *mushroom* hunters that is."

Jones nearly fell off her seat in relief. She wasn't quite sure what she was so worried about. I mean, if they were real ghost hunters, with any abilities whatsoever, they would have spotted Autumn as soon as they walked in. But hearing those words come out of Hugo's mouth was the last thing she was expecting.

"Ghost mushrooms?' asked Mr Manowski.

"Yes, apparently they're mushrooms that glow green at night," Hugo explained. "They usually only come out in winter, but because it's been so wet, everyone is very excited because a patch of ghost mushrooms has been found in the pines out at Mr Geier's. For the last week or so he's been hosting Ghost Mushroom Tours, and this is today's lot." Hugo flicked his tea towel towards the crowd in the dining area.

"They've arrived at lunchtime for a night tour?" Jones looked around the room, making more sense of the scene in front of her.

"I'm told they're making a day of it!" said Hugo. "I'm not complaining. The last week has been the busiest in the bar so far, and there are still a few more days to go before the last tour."

"Well, we best let you get back to it then!" said Jones. "Thank you, Hugo." Hugo smiled, nodded and moved across the bar to his next customer.

"Ghost mushrooms?" said Mr Manowski, "I've lived in the Hills my whole life, and I've never heard of them"

"Me either!" said Jones. "But they must be quite impressive considering the number of people here."

Mr Manowski grunted, emptied his glass of vodka and then hopped down from his stool.

"Thank you, Miss, oh! I'm terribly sorry, I don't know your name," he said.

"Jones," she said. "Jones Eldershaw. I run The Memory Bank."

"Of course," said Mr Manowski, extending his hand. "Lovely to meet you Miss Eldershaw." Jones took his hand and shook it. "I believe

I may have met your sister once or twice, but I certainly knew your father."

"You did?" Jones asked. Autumn was now standing next to Mr Manowski, and Jones quickly glanced her way.

"Oh yes," said Mr Manowski. "We used to chat at the pub back in the day. A lovely man." With that, he nodded his goodbye and walked out the door.

Jones's eyes followed Mr Manowski. There were certainly a lot of interesting people she was yet to meet in Lilly Pilly Creek, and Jones had a feeling she was going to be glad she met Mr Manowski. Then her stomach sunk as she remembered the circumstances of their meeting. Jones looked at Autumn.

"I hope Iris is going to be ok."

CHAPTER 6

Autumn didn't surprise Jones with a wake-up call the next morning, having stayed overnight in The Memory Bank as usual, and Jones enjoyed a small sleep-in. She had spent the rest of the previous afternoon in The Memory Bank, typing up Iris's interviews in between serving customers. There had been no update on Iris, and Jones found every time she was on the verge of sleep, the image of Iris, unconscious on the floor, her wedding dress splayed around her, would flash in her mind. It wasn't until early morning that Jones had managed to fall into a deep sleep, and as she pulled herself out of bed, all she could think about was a cup of Sybil's coffee.

Looking out the window it was another grey day, but fortunately, the rain was holding off for now. After dressing Jones went downstairs to make herself a serving of cheesy scrambled eggs on sourdough toast. She chopped some chives on top, and sat at the kitchen island, looking out into the garden. Despite the unseasonal weather, the garden appeared to be appreciating the wet, as the roses had started to make a vibrant appearance, in between some emerging foxgloves and Geraldton wax.

Jones was dying to message Drew to find out how Iris was, but she felt that may be overstepping their relationship. She had only met him once when she interviewed him for the Memory Box and collected a few items he wanted to include. He was a quiet man who she could tell truly loved Iris. A farmer, it was a little hard to draw out information from him, but when he shared the story of how they met when Iris joined the Lilly Pilly Creek Progress Society, Jones hadn't needed to say a word. She just let him speak, noticing the sparkle in his eye. Jones could only imagine how he was feeling now.

Popping her dishes into the dishwasher and turning it on, Jones grabbed her rain jacket and pulled it over the jumper she was wearing today, which said *'What is it with men and asking for directions?'* spoken wisely by Dory in Finding Nemo. She stepped outside, braced herself, and made her way to Sybil's.

From a distance, Jones could see that Sybil was wearing one of her classic outfits. Today it was a green beret on her grey hair, paired with a rain jacket covered in Van Gough's 'Starry Starry Night'.

As soon as Sybil spotted Jones she started waving at her to hurry over.

"What is it, Sybil?" Jones was worried. A few people were milling around, but Sybil made it clear she needed to talk with Jones urgently.

"Come round the back," Sybil said, wiping her hands on her apron and indicating to Jones to follow her behind the coffee van.

"I didn't want everyone else to hear," said Sybil, her voice lower than usual when Jones got to her. "I hear you were with Iris Wainwright when she collapsed?"

"Yes," said Jones. "Yes, I was. It was awful. Why? Do you know something?"

"Poison!"

"Poison?" Jones's mouth gaped.

"Yes! I heard from a nurse at the hospital. He said they suspect Iris was poisoned."

"You mean someone intentionally tried to hurt her?" Jones knew her face had turned white. It was the last thing she had expected to hear.

"Well, of that they can't be sure. I guess it could have been an accident, but it is certainly very suspicious." Sybil wrapped her arms around her body. "Not that I could imagine who would want to hurt poor Iris. She is such a lovely girl."

"But Sybil, why are we whispering behind your van?" asked Jones. Jones glanced around herself, feeling like she and Sybil were doing something untoward.

"Because I was told this in the strictest confidence," whispered Sybil. "My nurse friend could lose his job if anyone found out. So please, keep it to yourself. At least until the rest of the town starts passing the secret around." Sybil raised her eyebrow with a smile. They both knew what small towns were like, and it wouldn't be long before everyone was talking about Iris being poisoned.

"Of course, I'll keep it to myself," said Jones. "But why tell me?"

"Well," said Sybil. "You were there of course, and you're the detective, aren't you?"

Jones gasped. How did Sybil know that she and Autumn joked about being the Eldershaw Sisters Detective Agency? Had she overheard her?

"What do you mean?" Jones turned her head slightly, unsure of what Sybil would say.

"Why because you solved Autumn's murder of course! And when the police couldn't," Sybil said loudly, before lowering her voice again.

"And because, if the police need help this time, well, I just think you should have all the information they have." With a wink, Sybil walked back towards the front of the coffee van. "The usual?"

"Yes please, Sybil."

Jones felt somewhat bewildered. Is that what the town thought? That she solved Autumn's murder when the police couldn't? It wasn't true, was it? Jones felt sure the police would have been able to solve the murder, they just hadn't considered the idea in the first place. But Jones had to admit, without her, and Autumn herself, it may have been too late by the time the police decided to get themselves involved. By that time, they would have likely been solving two murders.

CHAPTER 7

Jones felt decidedly rude when Sybil served her instead of all the other people that had been waiting at the coffee van before her, but she was grateful as it meant she could hurry to The Memory Bank and hopefully share this news with Autumn before it hit the nine o'clock opening time.

The idea that Iris had been deliberately poisoned was shocking to Jones. She didn't want to believe it, but then she wondered, *could* it have been an accident? How hard was it to be accidentally poisoned? When it came to kids, it was certainly more common, but how often did you hear of an adult being accidentally poisoned? It seemed a very old-fashioned tragedy, not something that could happen in Lilly Pilly Creek today.

Jones rushed past Prue Timberley's real estate office, before crossing at the lights and walking in front of The Lilly Pilly Pantry. The black and white umbrellas were still down at this time of day, but she expected it wouldn't be long before people were sitting outside enjoying a snack, even on such a cool day. Finally, she passed Hugo's Wine Bar. Only the lights in the window were on. It appeared Hugo may be having a slow morning as well.

Quickly, Jones unlocked the front door walked in, and locked the door behind. "Autumn!" she called as she keyed in the alarm code.

Autumn appeared rapidly through a set of bookshelves to the left.

"What?" Autumn exclaimed. "What is it?"

"You're not going to believe this," said Jones. "But you've got to keep it a secret!"

Autumn laughed. "Who am I going to tell?" Jones realised her mistake and couldn't help but chuckle.

"Well, *anyway*, I've just been to Sybil's."

"And Sybil told you something, right?"

"How did you know?" asked Jones, genuinely surprised.

"Because Sybil always knows the town's secrets," said Autumn. "And you've burst in here like you've seen a ghost." Autumn raised one eyebrow at her joke.

"Fair enough," said Jones. She walked behind the counter and perched herself on one of the old leather bank stools her Grandparents had fortunately kept when they bought the Bank. "But seriously, you are not going to believe this. Sybil says that she's been told Iris was poisoned."

"No!" Autumn was as shocked as Jones had been.

"Yes!" said Jones. "At least that's what Sybil's nurse friend has told her."

"Are we thinking this is now looking rather suspicious?" asked Autumn, looking intently at Jones.

"It does seem to be quite suspicious, don't you think?"

Before Jones could say any more, a loud banging came from the front door.

"Someone's keen!" said Autumn, whisking herself over to the door and poking her head through.

"It's the police!" said Autumn.

"Is it really?" asked Jones, rushing over to open the door.

"Yes, it's Sergeant Schmidt himself."

Jones pulled out her key, unlocked the door and greeted Sergeant Christopher Schmidt. The two had met numerous times, including the time Jones discovered Autumn's death had not been an accident as the police originally presumed.

"Good morning Sergeant Schmidt," said Jones. "Is everything alright?"

"Good morning Miss Eldershaw," said Sergeant Schmidt. "Would it be ok if I came in for a moment? I just need a moment of your time to discuss what happened yesterday."

"Sure," said Jones. "Not a problem. Under one condition?"

Autumn spluttered at this, and Sergeant Schmidt raised his eyebrows. "And what would that be?"

"Could we use our first names? I don't know who you're talking to when you call me Miss Eldershaw. And if it was ok, it's much easier to say Chris than Sergeant Schmidt all the time." Jones smiled at the police officer, for a second wondering if she had overstepped the mark.

"Christopher," he responded. "I've always been called Christopher for some reason."

"Christopher, seriously?" Autumn said, floating ahead and making a point of rolling her eyes at Jones, a grin on her face.

"Perfect! Come in Christopher!" Jones waved him in, ignoring her sister. "Shall I lock the door again?"

"I think we should be ok," Christopher said. "I'm only going to be a few minutes. I just wanted you to explain to me what happened with Iris yesterday. I believe you were there?"

"Yes," said Jones, who took this opportunity to ask a question of her own. "Is Iris ok? I thought she just collapsed from being unwell. I'm surprised the police are involved."

"Nice one," said Autumn. "Totally innocent."

Christopher narrowed his eyebrows. "I ah can't really say," he said. "Although I imagine a police visit combined with the inevitable town gossip means you're putting two and two together. Let's just say, I need to investigate every lead at this stage."

Jones nodded, having no problem reading between the lines. "Oh, poor Iris."

"You were there weren't you?" asked Christopher. "When she collapsed?

"Yes," said Jones. "It was just awful. She'd just been telling me that she'd been unwell the past week, but was finally feeling better."

"So she seemed ok when you saw her?" Christopher was making notes as Jones spoke.

"Yes," said Jones. "Although, I couldn't say she looked one hundred per cent. Shadows under her eyes, and she just looked a bit, what do they say, green around the gills?"

Christopher nodded, taking notes. "But she told you she had been sick? For a week?"

"I think that was right," said Jones. "She said something to the effect that she was a week behind in her wedding preparations because she'd been unwell."

"Ok," said Christopher. "And, I do have to ask, why were you there?" He looked up, waiting for Jones's answer. If Jones didn't know better, she would have thought Christopher was investigating *her*. Autumn clearly agreed, calling out "How dare he!" Jones avoided even as much as a glimpse at her sister. If Christopher had even the slightest concern that Jones was involved in this, she most certainly didn't want to be seen interacting with an invisible being.

"To pick up some items for her memory box," said Jones. "Which I now realise I didn't even take!"

"Memory box?" asked Christopher, clearly confused.

"Oh, it's one of our lockboxes, filled with memories of Iris and Drew's family and friends," explained Jones. "It's going to be like a time capsule, to be presented to them at their wedding. I've also interviewed lots of their friends and family to create a memory book. Although that is still a work in progress."

Jones saw Christopher's eyebrows raise as he heard this. "You've interviewed everyone?" he asked.

"Sure have! It's been quite a project the last few weeks," she replied. She couldn't resist catching Autumn's eye. As she spoke it occurred to Jones that if Christopher was investigating the possibility that Iris was deliberately poisoned, her interviews may be a crucial part of the investigation.

"Interesting," he said. He appeared to mark his most recent note with a large asterix. Glancing at Autumn, Jones tried to tilt her head, indicating that now might be the perfect time to peer over Christopher's shoulder. Autumn returned Jones's expressions with a look of confusion.

"What are you talking about?" Autumn asked. Jones rolled her eyes and attempted to discreetly indicate note writing in the hope Autumn would understand.

"I think I have everything I need." Christopher snapped his notebook shut and looked up at Jones.

"Oh! The notebook," Autumn finally worked out what Jones had been trying to tell her. "Sorry, sorry. I'll catch it next time."

Jones ignored her sister and responded to Christopher. "Everything?" Jones was surprised he didn't immediately ask her for a copy of the interviews.

"For now," said Christopher, a slight smile on his face. "If I think we need to pursue things further, I will be in touch about those interviews."

Jones grinned at him. She couldn't put anything past him it seemed.

"So, I'll see you around," said Christopher. He nodded at Jones and started making his way to the front door.

"Yes, I suppose you will," said Jones, a little unsure what he meant. "I hope you work out what has happened."

Christopher pulled the door open to find customers on the doorstep. He nodded at them and left The Memory Bank.

"Good morning!" Jones called. "Come in Gladys! Come in Neha!!" She greeted two older ladies who often popped into The Memory Bank to buy some of the watercolour paints Jones had started stocking. She found that many people were using the good-quality notebooks she sold for their artwork, so it made sense to add a small selection of paints to their shelves. It was proving popular, at least with Gladys and Neha.

"Thank you, Jones," said Neha, holding a large satchel over her arm and peering at Jones. "We weren't sure if you'd be open this morning?"

"Oh," said Jones. "Why's that?" Jones tried to remember if today was a special day and drew a blank.

"Well, with all the drama at Mr Manowski's yesterday," said Gladys. "We heard you caught Iris as she fell!"

Autumn burst out in a peal of laughter. The grapevine was working its magic. Jones couldn't help but smile slightly, although it felt wrong when they were discussing a person who had potentially been poisoned in mysterious circumstances.

"No, no," said Jones. "I didn't catch her. I kind of wish I did. But I was there. It was all very sudden. I hope she's ok."

"Was Sergeant Schmidt here investigating?" Neha asked.

"Investigating?" said Jones, attempting to appear nonchalant by adjusting some pen jars on one of the tables. "No, Christoper just needed to confirm a couple of things. Normal in these circumstances I think."

"Oh, he's Christopher now, is he," Autumn said in her sing-song voice. Jones recognised she was implying something, but was unsure exactly what.

"*I* heard that it doesn't appear to be a normal circumstance at all," said Gladys, looking at her friend with a nod.

"Not at all," said Neha. "They're saying she was poisoned! That someone tried to kill her!"

Jones held back her desire to roll her eyes. Of course, she shouldn't be surprised. Gossip got around the town rather quickly. And she couldn't deny that as soon as she heard the word poison, the possibility of someone trying to murder Iris had certainly crossed her mind. Christopher's visit today seemed almost to confirm it.

"Well," said Jones. "I haven't heard a thing about that. All I know is she collapsed and was rushed to hospital. Has anyone heard how she's doing?"

Although she wanted to get to the bottom of the mystery, one way or another, Jones also realised Iris's welfare was more important than gossiping with two customers in her shop. Iris had become something of a friend to Jones over the past few weeks, and she would hate to think of something terrible happening to her, deliberate or otherwise.

"Still unconscious I'm told," said Neha.

"The poor dear," said Gladys, before finally asking about paints as though that was, of course, the real reason for their visit. "Now Jones, did you end up getting in any of the Gansai Watercolour Sets?

"Yes, I did actually," said Jones. "The Vintage and the 18 palette sets came in last week. They're over here." Jones took them over to the paint area before leaving them to mull over their purchases.

Autumn moved quickly to Jones's side. "We need to talk."

CHAPTER 8

"Why do you sound so concerned?" Jones asked Autumn when Neha and Gladys finally left The Memory Bank. As always, the pair couldn't resist a buy-up, and both took home one each of the new watercolour sets, along with more brushes and some sketchbooks. The two women may gossip a little too much for Jones's liking, but she couldn't deny they were loyal customers.

"I'm not concerned," said Autumn. "It's just, don't you think your interviews may hold some pretty important information?"

"I would hope so," said Jones. "That was the intention."

Autumn sighed. "I'm sure you've done a great job. But you know that's not what I mean."

Jones smiled. She quite liked teasing her sister, and this time it had worked like a charm. "You think my interviews might hold some clues to what has happened to Iris?"

"Exactly!" Autumn spun dramatically in front of Jones before floating back down to floor level. "So, what do you think? Do you think someone tried to *murder* Iris?"

Jones shook her head, not in denial, but in sadness. Ever since Sybil had told her Iris had been poisoned she couldn't ignore the fact that it was most likely deliberate. At least, the possibility couldn't be ignored before it was investigated thoroughly.

"I'm beginning to feel like The Eldershaw Detectives may have another case," Jones sighed.

Autumn clapped her hands, clearly excited by this new

development. She spun quickly in the air and was suddenly wearing a trench coat and fedora.

Jones laughed before saying, "Autumn, this is only happening because there may have been an *attempted murder*. Plus, the police seem to be on the case, this time. We may be of no real assistance whatsoever."

"Do you truly think that?" said Autumn. "Remember last time. Who was it that solved the murder? The Eldershaw Sisters Detective Agency! And who has likely interviewed every crucial person in this new case? You! It would be remiss of us to not at least review the information we already have."

Jones couldn't disagree. She'd only just started pulling the interviews into some sort of comprehensible document, but already she was casting her mind back to the conversations she'd had and the time spent with the various people in Iris and Drew's life.

"I have to be honest," said Jones. "Drew's family didn't seem to be that impressed with Iris. Or at least, they did bring up Drew's ex-girlfriend rather a lot."

"Tara, the ex-girlfriend who's the head winemaker at Casa Galati where Drew's brother is the head chef *and* Iris consumed her last meal? That ex-girlfriend?" Autumn tilted her head and raised her eyebrows, obviously trying to make a point. Hearing it said aloud, Jones realised even that simple connection seem rather suspicious, now that Iris was lying unconscious in the hospital.

"Yes, that ex-girlfriend," said Jones. "I think the whole family, in particular Drew's mother, was rather holding a candle to her. Davina,

Drew's mother, spoke a lot about Drew, about his brother Harris, about Tara, but spoke very little of Iris."

"She sounds like a charming person," said Autumn, rolling her eyes.

"I didn't think much of it at the time," said Jones. "It's funny how anything can become suspicious when a potential crime has occurred."

"Well, to experienced detectives like us at least," said Autumn, and the two sisters laughed.

"Solving one murder does not experienced detectives make!" said Jones.

"What else?" asked Autumn. "Is there anything more you feel is significant?"

"I'm not sure," said Jones. "I think we have to consider her fiancé, Drew."

"Obviously," said Autumn. "Always the first suspect."

"Exactly," said Jones. "Although, he does seem like a lovely guy and appears to truly love Iris.

"Anyone else?"

"Perhaps Drew's parents? If they weren't happy with the marriage," Jones suggested.

"And possibly Harris," suggested Autumn. "Maybe he thought it would be better for him if Drew married his boss instead. Then the winery would have a family connection?" Autumn shrugged.

"Worth pondering," Jones agreed. "Now, what about Iris herself? Could there possibly be anyone in her world outside of Drew and his family that would want to hurt her?"

"I spoke to her parents over the phone because they live in Goolwa, and I also met her brother Charlie. Now he is an interesting character."

"You did mention there was something a little unusual about him," said Autumn. "What was it again?"

"He's agoraphobic," said Jones.

"Agoraphobic? Is that when you're afraid of the outside?"

"Something like that," said Jones. "I imagine it's different for different people, but from what I've heard, Charlie has barely left the farm since he was in high school."

"Really? How old is he now?" Autumn was hovering in front of Jones, clearly very intrigued by the brother, Charlie.

"I think he's in his mid-thirties. He's a few years older than Iris," said Jones. "Aside from being a bit quirky, he seemed nice. Quite gentle. Very caring, especially with Iris. He talked a lot about looking after Iris when she was sick. The care in his voice was quite emotional. He must be so upset now that Iris is in the hospital."

"I can only imagine how hard it was for him," said Autumn. "Seeing your sister sick with cancer. You don't forget a thing like that."

"No, that is a memory that stays with you forever," said Jones.

The front door opened and Atlas walked in.

"Atlas!" said Jones. "Are you supposed to be working today?'

Atlas strode over, shaking his head. "No, it's ok. You haven't forgotten anything. I just," he glanced down at the floor before looking at Jones again. "I wanted to run an idea past you."

CHAPTER 9

Atlas moved to stand over near Jones, next to the collection of candles and photo frames they had available on a gift table. She was very curious to hear what Atlas had to say.

"Oh. An idea?" said Jones, tilting her head. "What idea was that?"

Autumn was pursing her lips, equally intrigued.

"Ok, so, you know how I've been running my own business on the side?" said Atlas.

"Yes, on the side of studying and working here," said Jones.

"Exactly!" Atlas nodded as though this explained everything.

"Not that I have any idea what your business is," Jones admitted.

"That's fine," said Atlas. "It's pretty boring computer stuff. The thing is, I've come up with a plan which I am hoping will work for both of us."

"Sounds good to me," said Jones. "What is it?"

"Well, as you know, I've been helping out in The Memory Bank quite a bit, when you're not available," Atlas explained.

"Oh is it too much!" Jones suddenly felt very concerned she had overstepped the mark with Atlas. "I realise I may have asked you to fill in one too many times. I can stop!"

Atlas laughed. "That's not it! You know I love working here. And I'm happy to fill in as much as you like. That's what I wanted to talk to you about. I've come up with a way that I can do my work and study *and* work here as much or as little as you need."

"This is sounding too good to be true," Jones smiled. "I cannot possibly imagine how!"

"Would you mind following me?" Atlas asked, indicating that he wanted to walk past the central counter to the back of the Bank building.

Atlas led Jones to one of the glassed-in rooms that used to be the Bank Manager's office. Now it wasn't used much. It was meant to be a backup if the other two small offices used for people to open or update their lockboxes were full. It wasn't ideal though, as two sides were completely glass, so there was no real privacy.

Atlas turned around to face Jones. "What would you think if I rented this room from you and turned it into my business office?" Atlas tipped his head, clearly unsure how Jones was going to react to his suggestion. "That way I'll be here a lot more, working, and if you ever need me to fill in or help when things get busy, we'll I'm right here."

"Oh Atlas," said Jones, clasping her hands in front of herself. "I think this is a brilliant idea!"

Atlas broke out into a wide grin. "I'm so relieved," said Atlas. "I thought you would think it was ridiculous!"

"It's a genius idea," Autumn piped in, causing Jones to smile.

"Yes, it's a genius idea," said Jones. "I love it. Absolutely!"

"What's a genius idea?" A voice called from behind them. It was Jones's best friend Wren.

"Atlas is going to open an office right here in The Memory Bank!" Jones declared, turning to face Wren.

"Really?" said Wren. "That *is* a great idea!"

"I'm going to rent the room from Jones," said Atlas. "And then I'll be here to help when she needs me outside of my normal shifts."

"That sounds like a complicated lease agreement," said Wren, putting her lawyer hat on.

Jones laughed. "Trust you, Wren. I think Atlas and I can keep it simple enough." She turned to Atlas. "We'll sit down and ensure it's fair, but I imagine there would be weekly rent, and then whatever you work for me beyond your shifts, we could deduct from your rent. Or I just pay you the extra?"

"If you want my advice," said Wren, who was going to offer it anyway. "Keep the office rent and the employee pay separate. It will get too complicated at tax time otherwise."

Atlas shrugged in agreement. "Sounds simple enough."

"I'm happy to draw up a basic agreement for you both if you like?" offered Wren.

"That would be lovely," said Jones. "Thank you."

Wren and Atlas walked into the office, just as Jones's phone started ringing.

"Hello?"

"Ah herm, uh, this is Charlie," said a deep voice on the other end of the line. "Charlie Wainwright. Iris's brother."

"Hi Charlie," said Jones. "How can I help you? How's Iris?"

Jones heard a sniff and was immediately concerned the worst had happened. Fortunately, her hunch was wrong.

"Still unconscious. They are treating her but can't say if it will help," he explained. Jones could hear sniffing and gulping and it was clear Charlie was crying although trying his best to restrain himself.

"Is there anything I can do?" Jones asked.

"My pictures," he said. "I want my pictures back."

"Your pictures?" Jones couldn't work out what he was talking about.

"Yes, my pictures," Charlie responded shortly. He sounded very distressed which, under the circumstances, probably shouldn't be surprising. "The ones I gave you. My pictures."

Jones realised that it was obvious what he was talking about. "Your pictures in the Memory Box? Of course, you can have them back. Did you want to pick them up?"

The phone went silent. It took a moment for Jones to realise what she had said. "Or perhaps I could come out to you? I imagine you need to stay by the phone, just in case there's news about Iris."

Autumn raised her eyebrows and Jones poked her tongue out in return. She knew the concept of staying near the phone was completely ridiculous in the day and age of mobile phones, but she was doing her best to give Charlie an out, without embarrassing him.

"Thank you, yes," said Charlie. "If you could bring them to me, today, that would be greatly appreciated."

Wren and Atlas had now walked back out into the room and were silently waiting for Jones.

"I'll pull it out of the Memory Box shortly, and bring it round to you after closing time if that suits?"

"Yes," said Charlie. "Yes, thank you. I will be at the house waiting." With that, he hung up.

"Who was that?" asked Wren. Jones found it a little forward for Wren to ask about a private conversation, but she told her anyway.

"It was Charlie, Iris's brother. He wants me to drop something to him."

"Something from the Memory Box you've been working on?" Wren asked, scrunching her eyebrows.

"Yes," Jones replied. "Some pictures, drawings I think, he did for Iris."

"I"m not sure that's such a good idea," said Wren.

Jones was surprised. Why shouldn't Charlie ask for his belongings back? Maybe he wanted to take them to Iris in the hospital. "Why not?"

"They could be evidence," said Wren.

"Really? Evidence?" The thought had not even crossed Jones's mind.

"Of course!" said Autumn. "The whole Memory Box might be filled with evidence!"

"Yes," said Wren. "I wouldn't be touching anything until you check with the police.

"With Christopher," Autumn piped in unhelpfully, eyes sparkling.

"Evidence of what?" asked Atlas. Jones realised Atlas would have been the last person to be on the end of the community grapevine.

Wren turned to Jones. "Look, I can't say anything," said Wren. "Because I've found out about this via one of my clients, so it's confidential."

"You have?" asked Jones.

"Yes," said Wren. "So, I won't say anything, but if you've heard anything, you can pass it on to Atlas. You're not bound by client privilege."

Jones nodded and turned to Atlas, telling him everything she knew so far about Iris, the poisoning, and the fact that it may be a criminal case.

"Sergeant Schmidt has already been to see you?" asked Wren, genuinely surprised. "So they *do* think something's suspicious?"

"Should I have said that?" asked Jones. "Or was I supposed to keep it confidential, that Christopher had been to ask me questions?"

"Christopher?" said Wren. "You're allowed to call him by his first name?"

"Why is that so surprising?" asked Jones. "Don't you? I imagine you talk to him all the time."

"I can't think of anyone who calls him by his first name," replied Wren.

With that Jones went a little red. She realised she'd demanded she call him by his first name. Perhaps she'd said something wrong. She would call him Sergeant Schmidt from now on.

"That might be my fault," said Jones. "I sort of insisted."

"And he let you? Well, that is a first." Wren smiled at Jones, an expression she couldn't quite read. "Anyway, back to Charlie. What you've said makes it even more important that you don't distribute any of the items from that Memory Box until you've confirmed with Sergeant Smith, *Christopher*." Wren emphasised the last word with a grin. "That it isn't needed as evidence."

"Yes, I'm sure you're right," said Jones. "I'll visit the police station first before I do anything further."

CHAPTER 10

"The only one who calls him Christopher," hissed Autumn after Wren left. Jones was walking towards Atlas's proposed office so they could discuss details.

"So?" said Jones, under her breath. "What's the problem? Aside from the fact that I may have been quite rude and forced his hand."

"He's a police officer for goodness sake," said Autumn. "Do you think he would have allowed you to call him Christopher if he didn't *want* you to?"

"Well, maybe he's relaxing his rules? Maybe it's just around lawyers like Wren that he prefers to remain formal?" Jones honestly didn't know what Autumn was going on about. All of this sounded perfectly reasonable to Jones.

"Yeh, right," Autumn said, the sarcasm dripping from her tongue.

"So Atlas," said Jones, walking away from Autumn and through the doorway. "Congrats on your new office!"

Atlas was sitting in a swivel chair that was kept in the office. He spun to face her, grinning. He was pleased with their new arrangement.

"Thanks, Jones," said Atlas. "I can't believe I have my very own proper office!"

"It is pretty cool," said Jones. "What sign are you going to put on the door?" Jones indicated the door to the room they were standing in.

"Sign?" asked Atlas, frowning.

"You know," said Jones. "Your business name. You want to let people know where to find you, right?"

"Do you think? Wow, that would be just like a real business." Atlas stared at the door, clearly imagining the possibilities.

"It is a real business, isn't it?" said Jones. She had no idea what his business was.

"Oh yes, of course," said Atlas. "It's just I've been running it out of my bedroom for two years. Now, with an office, it's like I've moved to the big time!"

"Well, I'm glad I can be a part of it," said Jones. "Now, not to push the new arrangement too far too soon, but would you be able to work from about four and then close up? It sounds like I'm going to need to make a trip to the police station before I get back to Charlie."

"Of course!" Atlas said, standing and putting his hands on his hips. "You can count on me. I might just stay until then, so I can also start measuring up and working out what furniture I'll need."

"Perfect," said Jones. "And help yourself to any of the furniture in storage. If it's your style of course."

"Are you going to come with me?" Jones asked Autumn when she was sure she was out of earshot. She could hear Atlas with his tape measure. He had come prepared, hopeful Jones would agree.

"Where?" said Autumn, who had decided now was the time to demonstrate to Jones that she could float on her side, arm bent, hand under her chin, like she was laying on a bed or couch. When Jones's eyes boggled, Autumn, straight-faced, slowly floated upright. "To the police station, or Charlie's?"

"Both?" said Jones. "Or is that pushing you too far?"

"Where does he live? How far out of town?" Autumn lowered herself to the ground and extended her arms out to her side, twisting her hands at the wrist. To Jones, it appeared as though Autumn was testing how much energy she had in and around her body.

"I think it's about three kilometres," said Jones. "Probably a bit too far." She shared a concerned look with her sister.

"Why don't we give it a whirl?" said Autumn. "We'd drive, wouldn't we? Then we can race back if we need to."

"Are you sure?" said Jones. "Isn't it a bit risky?" Her stomach clenched. Any time Autumn's energy dropped even a little Jones panicked that her sister would disappear forever. Neither of them had any idea what would happen if her energy dropped too low. Jones personally did not want to find out. This ghost business was new, to both of them. No Google search would provide the answers. The two of them were winging it alone, and the idea of losing Autumn again, forever, meant taking such a gamble was simply too much for Jones.

"I think we need to try," said Autumn. "I've been feeling really good lately. Stronger. My trip home by myself barely impacted me." She twirled, her skirt dancing around her legs, having now removed the coat and hat.

"Barely," said Jones. "But home is nothing in comparison to three kilometres," said Jones.

"Let's try," said Autumn. "This is an Eldershaw Detective Agency Job after all. I'm crucial to the team."

Jones couldn't deny that she would be glad to have Autumn with her at Charlie's. Charlie seemed to be a kind, gentle sort of person, but the intensity with which he spoke to her on the phone earlier meant she was slightly apprehensive about the visit. At least it should be a quick drop-and-go.

Jones spent the next few hours serving customers and also decided she was going to rearrange some of the display tables, with Autumn's guidance. As they'd had quite a bit of new stock arrive recently, she thought grouping them by activity rather than type of product would work well. Jones was surprised at how much fun she was having and was shocked when Autumn told her it was already a quarter to four.

"Well, I'd better grab the memory box then, hadn't I," said Jones.

Jones walked back to the lockbox room. It was filled with the original numbered safety deposit boxes, many now containing the memories of their clients, carefully stored in the Bank. Nothing of great value, such as jewellery or legal documents, could be stored in them these days, as The Memory Bank didn't have quite the same level of security as a real bank. Their customers stored such things as journals, photos, letters, and their memoirs. It was a service The Memory Bank was known for and it was loved by everyone who used it.

The security at The Memory Bank had been slightly increased recently, since Jamie, Autumn's ex-boyfriend who was responsible for pushing her down the Bank's spiral staircase, was caught breaking in. The front door had a new lock, still in the old-fashioned style "in keeping with the history" as Jones had insisted, plus the alarm system that had now been installed. The security company had tried to encourage Jones to install security cameras, but she felt that was going one step too far. She didn't want her customers feeling watched as they strolled around the Bank, and they most certainly couldn't have them in the rooms where people placed their most treasured and private memories into their lockboxes. The Memory Bank considered confidentiality of the highest importance, and Jones wouldn't jeopardise that for anything.

Jones turned her attention to the lockbox she was trying to retrieve. As they all were, it was secured behind its own numbered door. Placing a small silver key in the lock, it clicked open and she was able to pull the door open. Tugging on the little handle at its end, Jones slid the lockbox most of the way out, before gripping the box and hefting it onto the wooden table behind her.

It would be quite awkward to transport the lockbox. They weren't designed to be easily taken out of the Bank, if at all. Jones considered emptying Iris and Drew's Memory box, but what else would be secure? Instead, she found a strong canvas bag to put the lockbox in. She believed the bag was one used by shops in the past to bring their daily takings to the Bank. Jones placed it into a small trolley that they sometimes used to transport items around the store when new stock had arrived. Jones thought she just might be able to get the Memory Box to the police station this way.

"Today's a day you wish you'd brought the car, isn't it?" said Autumn helpfully.

"Well, you're certainly no help," said Jones. "If you were alive we could have taken turns pulling!" Jones gulped when she realised what she had said. Autumn, however, laughed it off, shooting back her own barb.

"If I was still alive, you'd be in Adelaide chasing stories!" Autumn was grinning, but that comment did sting a little. Jones often felt guilt about the fact that it had taken Autumn's death for them to get as close as they were now. Autumn was right. If she was still alive, there is no way Jones would have been working at The Memory Bank. That was Autumn's thing. Jones's focus had been on her journalism career. And she still hadn't completely cut the cord. There was a job in Adelaide waiting for her whenever she wanted. Jones had pushed that decision to one side for now, having taken a year off without pay.

Jones wondered if she would ever return to The Advertiser, the newspaper she worked for. Would she work in journalism again? She supposed, technically, her interviews for Iris and Drew's Memory Box were exactly that. She was using her reporter skills to find the story. Although she hadn't taken the time to consider it properly, perhaps Wren was right all those weeks ago when she put the idea in Jones's head. Maybe she would find a way to combine journalism *and* The Memory Bank.

For now, Jones pulled the loaded trolley through the Bank, bumping noisily across the original timber floors, and attempted to get it down the front steps without too big a disaster.

"I'll help!" said Atlas, running up. He grabbed one end of the trolley whilst Jones grabbed the other, and carefully they guided it onto the footpath.

"Gee, that's heavier than it looks!" said Atlas.

"Tell me about it," said Jones. "Thanks, Atlas, and thanks for looking after the Bank."

"No, problems!" he said, as Jones trundled off down the street.

CHAPTER 11

Jones knew people were staring at her as she bumbled along, the Memory Box jolting every time the trolley hit a crack in the footpath.

"Do you think we should call all of the lockboxes, Memory Boxes?" asked Autumn. "I mean it seems obvious. Why didn't we do that before?"

"I was pondering that," said Jones, puffing slightly as she pulled. "But what I was thinking is that these Memory Boxes are more of a, shall we say, community box. This is where lots of people are depositing their memories for others to share. For a special occasion, like this one. At least, that's how I think we should market it."

"Market it hey?" said Autumn, gliding next to Jones, with absolutely no exertion whatsoever. "So a whole new product line?"

"I think so," said Jones. "I mean it was a brilliant idea from Iris and Drew."

"It certainly was," said Autumn.

Jones trundled across the traffic lights before turning and making her way towards the police station. The red brick building, with its bull nose verandah and screen door, looked just like someone's home, except for the large blue police sign on the front and all the notices stuck on the pinboard next to the door.

Autumn glided through before Jones even had a chance to pull the screen door open.

"It'd be nice to have a little help," Jones muttered as the trolley banged into the main wooden door. Eventually, Jones managed to pull the main wooden door open and lurched into the room.

"Oh, Miss Eldershaw, Jones, do you need some help?" Christopher lifted part of the counter he was behind and made his way into the room.

"I'm fine thanks, Sergeant Schmidt," said Jones. "I just thought you might need to see this."

"Christopher, remember?" he said with a slight smile on his face. "What is this you've brought in?"

"See!" said Autumn. "Only you!"

Jones knew her face was going red but she hurried into an explanation. "It's the Memory Box. The one I mentioned. For Drew and Iris. Wren thought you might want to see it?"

"Oh she did, did she?" Christopher was standing there with his arms crossed over his chest.

"Well, yes, you know, it might be evidence?" Jones raised her hands in a question. "It does contain mementos from all of their closest friends and family."

"Yes, I suppose she could be right," said Christopher. "Let's pop it up on the counter."

Autumn laughed as she saw Jones attempt to lift it from the trolley. Being almost at floor level, it was quite a challenge.

"Here, let me," said Christopher, moving to bend down opposite Jones, smiling at her. Jones heard Autumn's sharp intake of breath and glanced at her in panic. She was surprised to see her sister grinning at her. Jones stood up and shook her head slightly in her sister's direction, whilst Christopher managed to place the canvas bag containing the memory box onto the counter. He then turned to Jones, indicating that she should remove the bag.

Walking to the counter, Jones pulled the bag down and over the sides of the Memory Box. Taking out the key, she paused.

"Now, in normal circumstances, it would be completely against policy to open this and show it to anyone," said Jones. "But is Wren right? Could this be considered evidence?"

"Possibly," said Christopher. "Do you have any reason to believe it is?"

"No," said Jones. "Not really. It's just, when Wren was at The Memory Bank earlier, Charlie, Iris's brother, called me quite distressed, and asked if I could return the item he had placed in here. When I told Wren I was going to drop it off today, she cautioned me, thinking you'd want to see things first."

Christopher nodded. "She might be right. Charlie rang? Did he say how Iris was?"

"No change apparently," said Jones, shrugging. "Shall I open this?"

"Sure," said Christopher. "It is probably prudent to check it.

"What if it contains a little jar marked 'drink me'?" Autumn laughed.

Jones placed the silver key into the lock and clicked the box open. Inside was a slightly smaller wooden box which she pulled out and lifted the lid.

The box contained a collection of all the memories that had been shared with Drew and Iris, to open on their tenth wedding anniversary. Christopher, despite his scepticism, had pulled on a pair of gloves and started pulling out items, quickly analysing each one, before moving on to the next. Handwritten recipes, photos, pressed flowers, a bookmark, it contained a whole variety of things. Christopher looked over each item before placing it back in the box.

"I don't think there's anything much here," he said. "But I think it would be prudent if I were to take a quick photograph of everything before you return anything. Which item is Charlie's?"

Jones pointed at the largest item in the box, which only just fit. It was a manilla envelope and on the front was Iris's name with a beautiful drawing of an Iris flower. "Charlie drew that," said Jones. "I'm not exactly sure what else is in it, but I believe there are more drawings."

Christopher nodded. "I'm just going to take the Memory Box into the back room and take photos. I won't be a moment."

Jones nodded and watched him walk behind the counter and through the door into a back room. Of course, Autumn followed him. Jones took the opportunity to sit down. She had tried to hide it, but towing the memory box halfway through Lilly Pilly Creek had worn her out. Yet instead of thinking about Iris, Charlie, or the Memory Box, Jones found her thoughts turning to Christopher. Was it that strange that he had now clearly insisted she call him Christopher? Surely he was just being a nice person. Autumn could read anything into anything, she knew that. But was there more to it? And if there was, what did Jones think about that concept? She barely knew him, except in the context of her sister's murder investigation. He had always been very professional, to the point of being a little abrupt. This did seem to have changed in their most recent interactions, but was that just because Autumn's murder had now been solved? Could he now have more normal conversations around her?

Of course, that was it. It was ridiculous for anyone, especially Autumn, to think anything else. Meanwhile, she wondered what Autumn was noticing as she watched Christopher take the photographs. Jones would be surprised if there was anything in the Memory Box that could be considered evidence. There was nothing that she could recall, although she hadn't gone through the items in the box herself. That certainly wasn't her place.

"Wow," said Autumn, gliding back into the room. "Charlie's drawings are amazing!"

"Shh," said Jones. "We'll talk about it later."

"Did you know he was an artist?"

Jones shook her head as she heard the rear door opening. Christopher walked out with the Memory Box and started returning it to the bag.

"I'm not sure if it will be relevant," said Christopher. "But if these are items provided by all the important people in Iris and Drew's life, it's certainly worth having this information. It was smart of Wren to recommend you bring this in."

Jones looked at him. Christopher seemed to have changed his tune a little, since looking through the items. Perhaps there *was* something in the box. Jones glanced at Autumn, before pulling up the bag and reaching to lift it onto the trolley.

"Here," said Christopher. "Let me." He took the bag, placed it on the trolley, and smiled at Jones.

"Thanks," said Jones smiling back. "And it's ok if I return Charlie's pictures now?"

"It sure is," he replied. "But how are you getting there? What are you doing with this trolley?" Christopher lowered his eyes to the bulky set-up Jones had and then looked back at her.

"Oh, I'm just going to my house," said Jones. "Then I'll take my car to Charlie's farm."

"Come on," said Christopher. "Jump in my car and I'll whiz you home. It'll be quicker than trudging up the road with this!"

"No," said Jones. "I couldn't possibly!"

"Do it!" said Autumn.

"I'm going to have to insist," said Christopher. "What will people think if they see you struggling out the door with this?"

"What will they think seeing me get into a police car?" Jones responded with a slight tone of humour in her voice. Secretly she did want to get into that police vehicle. The thought of lugging that trolley all the way to her house, especially when the sky seemed to be darkening again outside, made her feel a little queasy.

Fortunately, Christopher ignored her weak protest and started pulling the trolley out the front door. Once Jones was through he quickly locked the door, before tugging the trolley to the police car parked at the back of the building. It was a four-wheel drive, emblazoned with blue lines and large letters spelling POLICE across all sides. She was going to have to resign herself to this potential embarrassment for the benefit of a quick and dry trip. At that moment, the rain started to fall in large heavy drops, encouraging Jones to rapidly jump into the car and shut the door.

"That was lucky," said Autumn. Jones turned to see her ghostly sister sitting in the back seat, smiling at her. Jones quickly turned to the front and buckled herself in as Christopher opened the door.

"Now, where's your house again?" he asked.

"Lemon Myrtle Street," Jones replied. "About halfway up."

The police car barked to life, and they made their way onto Lilly Pilly Creek's Main Street, as the rain beat down. Jones was thankful for the ride, even if it was in a police car. No one would notice her in this downpour anyway. They turned right onto Acacia Street and continued up the hill before turning left onto Lemon Myrtle Street.

"That one," Jones said, pointing to a gorgeous old stone home, surrounded by the cottage garden her mother had planted. Jones was doing her best to help it thrive again, but there was a reason her paying job didn't involve plants. Gardening most certainly wasn't her forte.

Christopher pulled the police four-wheel drive up behind Jones's car, a cream Mini Cooper with racing stripes on the bonnet. The comparison was striking.

"Ok if I leave everything by the front door?" said Christopher.

"Actually, in my boot if that's ok?"

"Sure," said Christopher, and he jumped out.

Jones followed him, desperately tugging her jacket up over her head in an attempt to block the rain. It had little effect, and she could feel her hair dripping across her face. Walking behind the car, Christopher had already grabbed out the box and the trolley and was now striding up the driveway towards her car. He graciously stood waiting as Jones fumbled with her keys, searching for the button to pop the boot. Placing both the box and the trolley inside, he looked at Jones and pointed. "Is that alright?" he called above the drumming of the rain

"Yes!" said Jones. "Thank you!"

"Not a problem!" Christopher replied. "I'll catch you later." He raced back, jumped in his car, and was reversing out of the driveway before Jones noticed Autumn standing next to her.

"That was very kind of him," said Autumn.

"Yes it was," said Jones. "Now get in!"

CHAPTER 12

Jones had only been to Charlie Wainwright's house once when she first went to pick up his envelope. She thought she remembered the way, but the rain made all the landmarks blur into an impressionist painting.

"The farm is on Blue Ridge Road," said Jones. "If I remember correctly, there's a stall out the front."

"A stall?" said Autumn.

"Yes," said Jones. "You know, one of those roadside stalls you see everywhere in the Hills. Selling veggies and flowers and things."

"Right, right," said Autumn, peering out the window, trying to spot anything that may resemble a stall.

"Isn't there something ghostly you can do to help?" asked Jones, driving slowly, and leaning over her steering wheel, as if that slightly shorter distance between herself and the windscreen was going to make any difference to her vision.

"Ghostly? What do you mean?"

"Oh, I don't know," Jones replied. "Can you make it so the windscreen stays clear of rain, or create some sort of clear weather tunnel in front of us?"

"I'm not a wizard, Jones!" Autumn laughed. "I don't have magical powers."

"Well you were able to break the window," said Jones. Jones was referring to the night Autumn saved her life. Whilst Jones was in a heated and dangerous situation in the tower at the top of the Memory

Bank, dragged up there by none other than Autumn's murderer, and ex-boyfriend, Jamie Royce, Autumn had managed to summon some sort of power that was enough for her to smash the Bank's front window and alert Hugo next door. It was Hugo who had then smashed his way in through the back, and raced up the stairs, pinning Jamie to the wall.

"Yes, the window," said Autumn. "I still don't know how I did that. I think it would have a connection to the situations where mothers lift cars off their children. Some overpowering adrenalin rush perhaps."

"And you haven't been able to do anything even remotely close since?"

"Nope! I haven't even been able to push a pencil on a table."

"It's just unbelievable that you were able to break the window that night. Think what may have happened otherwise." Jones shuddered, trying not to imagine the scenario Jamie had threatened her with.

"How sad it would be if Autumn's sister also accidentally fell down the staircase," he had said to her as he held her at the top of The Memory Bank's spiral staircase.

"Well, it's all ok now," said Autumn, turning to look at her sister, and they both shrugged. It wasn't exactly ok, what with Autumn being dead and all, but she had returned as a ghost, and for that, they were both very thankful. "Plus, the new window and sign look fantastic!"

"It does look good," said Jones. The window that Autumn had smashed had held the original gold logo of The Memory Bank. Over the long years it had lasted quite well, with a few touch-ups, but was a little worse for wear. It had now been replaced with the same logo, but the glow of the new gold was beautiful. Jones and Autumn had stood outside The Memory Bank, admiring it for a long time the day it was installed.

"I did use my ghostly powers today," said Autumn.

"You did?" Jones couldn't remember anything of particular note.

"That whole, walking through walls thing," Autumn laughed.

"Oh, you mean at the police station?" asked Jones. "Did you see anything?"

"No, not really," said Autumn. "Christopher was right. I don't think there's any real evidence in the memory box. But Charlie's drawings are amazing! Did you know he was an artist?"

"No, I had no idea," said Jones. "Is that what was in the envelope?"

"Yes!" said Autumn. "The most amazing botanical drawings of all sorts of flowers and fungi and moss and lots of things. Of course, there were a few different drawings of irises including I think a wild iris. It was very impressive."

"You just never know what hidden talents people have," said Jones.

"There it is!" called out Autumn, pointing to a large shape out in front.

"The stall! Great," said Jones. "Because I was beginning to think we'd missed it."

Jones indicated and carefully pulled her Mini Cooper into the driveway of "Twelve Oaks Farm".

"Oh my goodness!" Jones gasped. They had turned down the most stunning gravel driveway. The entire way was lined with ornamental pear trees, which were still in blossom, although the rain was assisting in removing many of the petals. Underneath, in a variety of shades from purple to deep red and even blush pink, were hundreds and hundreds of irises. It was stunning.

"Irises for Iris," said Autumn, very quietly. The two were silent as they slowly drove towards the farmhouse, taking in sight before them.

The gravel driveway swung to the left and took them directly to the entrance of the Twelve Oaks farmhouse. It was a large red brick home in a Tudor style, with a tiled roof and three striking triangular peaks across the front. A central archway marked the entrance, with a deep verandah on one side, and a substantial brick chimney on the other. It gave a grand impression and was very old, yet well-kept. This was a home that was loved.

"Twelve Oaks Farm is all very impressive," said Autumn as the two slid out of Jones's car, Jones tucking the package for Charlie into her jacket.

"It most certainly is," said Jones, taking her time, despite the rain, to stare up at the trim in the triangles that had been painted black to contrast with the white behind it. The steeply pitched roof, which overhung on all sides of the home, was quite unusual for The Adelaide Hills and harked back to the English countryside.

Jones walked to the front door and twisted the old-fashioned brass doorbell. The chirp of the bell could be heard on the other side of the door. Very quickly heavy, loud footsteps came towards them and the door was opened.

"Oh good, good," said a man, at the door. Charlie was very imposing, both broad and tall, with a head of faded blonde hair and a russet look to his cheeks. He was wearing a flannel shirt, well-worn jeans, and a striped apron over the lot. Without a word he stepped to the side, indicating for Jones to walk inside.

"Thank you, Charlie," said Jones, as she walked into the very wide entry hall of the home. "How is Iris?"

"Come through, come through," Charlie rushed down the hallway away from Jones. "Jam on the stove!" he called over his shoulder.

"Jam!" said Autumn. "Well, that explains the stall."

Jones walked down the long Persian runner and glanced at the many pictures and items hanging on the wall. Most were black and white photos, clearly charting the history of the home and the farm. There were also show ribbons of various types, along with many pieces of art. Here and there a solid piece of wooden furniture stood against the wall, beautifully polished, and sparsely decorated. All in very good taste.

"In here!" Charlie called. Jones turned to the right and fortunately took note of the step down into the large kitchen. Charlie's back was to them as he stirred a giant pot over the flame of a stove that looked as though it had been there since the house was built. White cupboards lined one wall, an oversized and well-loved kitchen table stood in the middle of the room, whilst pots, pans and other cooking implements hung from the ceiling in one corner. The kitchen was very clean and organised.

Jones placed the envelope on the table ensuring it lay in a clear, safe place.

"Almost done," said Charlie, not looking away from his pot.

"What type of jam is it?" asked Jones. She turned to look at Autumn, but she was gone. Obviously off 'investigating'.

"Strawberry and rhubarb," he replied. He had stopped stirring and was now just watching the pot. "One of Iris's favourites."

"Oh that's lovely," said Jones. "Something for when she gets better."

"Yes," said Charlie. "When she comes home, I'll have everything ready so I can look after her properly."

Jones frowned, a little surprised that Iris would be coming back to the farm once she was out of the hospital, but she supposed she would still consider it her home and might be more comfortable here with her family. Perhaps Drew would come to stay whilst she recovered.

"And she's doing ok?"

Finally, the jam appeared to be ready. Drew lifted the pot and placed it on the far side of the stove, before turning off the element. He turned to face Jones.

"I'm not sure," said Charlie. "Mum and Dad are there. They said she still isn't awake."

Jones found herself looking at a man distraught that his sister was so unwell. She felt an overwhelming desire to hug this tall, solid man and tell him everything would be ok. Of course, she had no idea if that was the case.

"Well," said Jones. "I hope the doctors work out what's happening and she comes home soon. Do you have any idea who might want to hurt Iris?"

Charlie's eyes widened. "Hurt her? No one! Who would ever want to hurt Iris?"

"Sorry," said Jones. "Sorry, I didn't mean to alarm you. You're probably right. It was probably an accident."

"Yes," said Charlie. "I'm sure it was. But I need to get back to my cooking. I've got a lot more to do before Iris comes home. I'm baking an apricot crumble next."

"Of course, I'll leave you to it." Jones turned and Charlie led her towards the front door.

As Jones walked down the hallway, she was shocked to see Autumn's translucent figure appear from under the floorboards in front of her. Jones couldn't help but make a sudden noise of shock.

"Are you ok?" asked Charlie.

Jones shook her head in frustration. "Yes, sorry, I'm fine. Just caught my toe." Typical for Autumn to appear in the most inappropriate way. Autumn on the other hand had a huge grin on her face, clearly quite proud of herself.

"Thank you," said Charlie. "Thank you for bringing my pictures." He pulled the door open, nodding slightly at Jones in farewell.

"Not a problem at all," said Jones, stepping out of the door. "If you need anything, you know you can call."

Charlie nodded again before closing the door. Jones could hear his heavy footsteps walking away.

"What a funny man," said Autumn. "Strange. A bit too strange?"

"What, you don't think?" Jones turned to Autumn, her mouth wide open.

Autumn shrugged. "I have no idea," she said. "But don't you think he gives off weird vibes?"

Jones had to admit she was right. But strange enough to attempt to kill his sister? And then whip up meals for her? Jones shook her head. She had no idea.

CHAPTER 13

Jones climbed back into her car. Autumn decided on a more dramatic entrance and slid through the roof directly onto her seat.

"Can you stop doing things like that!" said Jones. "You nearly scared me half to death in there. Charlie will think I'm losing my marbles."

"Oh come on," said Autumn. "You have to admit it was a bit hilarious."

Jones rolled her eyes. "But where exactly were you coming from? Straight through the ground?"

"Oh no. Although-" Autumn paused, clearly considering trying that. "No, I was coming from the cellar. Charlie has a stockpile down there, big enough to get through the apocalypse."

"Really?" said Jones. "What types of things?"

"Jams, chutneys, jars of preserved lemons, lots of dried herbs and things, like you know those delicious dried oranges and apples you have with your gin. A lot I had no idea what I was looking at, but he is clearly into his food."

"I wonder if he sells it?" asked Jones. "Aside from the stall of course. Perhaps Hugo could use it at the bar?"

"That's a pretty cool idea," said Autumn. "I'm sure he'd like some local products. Would any of it work in The Memory Bank? Or is extending to food a step too far?"

"Probably a step too far," said Jones. "But you never know, at one point we might have a local showcase or something. I've learnt so much about our little town in recent weeks, and people are doing amazing things."

"It seems like you've enjoyed preparing The Memory Box," said Autumn. "Getting back out there, interviewing people?"

Jones smiled and nodded. She was glad Autumn had been the one to bring it up. She hadn't wanted to admit to Autumn that being back in her journalist stride had been nice. Jones was concerned she may give her sister the impression that she was regretting reopening The Memory Bank.

"It has been fun, she replied. "And it's gotten me thinking."

"Oh yes?" Autumn turned to look at her sister, but Jones kept her eyes on the road, turning her car right off the dirt road and onto the bitumen that led into Lilly Pilly Creek. The road was lined with gum trees and wattle, the yellow fuzzy flowers bringing brightness to the grey day.

"There has to be a way that I can incorporate my journalism skills into The Memory Bank," she explained. "Wren was the first one to put the idea in my head and when Iris approached me about their Memory Box, well, it seems this could be one way of doing it. I don't think there would be a huge demand for Memory Boxes, at least not a project of this size. But is there something else I could do?"

"There has to be," said Autumn, putting her hand to her chin. "We're just going to have to start brainstorming. I'm sure a great idea will come to us."

Jones glanced at Autumn and then did a double take. Autumn seemed to have faded.

"Autumn!" Jones cried. "Are you ok?"

"What do you mean?" Autumn looked down at her hands and then lifted them, turning them. "Oh, I see what you mean."

"Will you be ok to get back to The Memory Bank? We're nearly there." Jones tried to keep herself calm, but she had never seen Autumn like this.

"I do feel a bit flat now that I think about it," said Autumn. "But I'm sure I'll be ok."

They drove past the 'Welcome to Lilly Pilly Creek' sign and slowed down, ready to turn left onto Main Street. The grey road glistened but finally, it seemed the rain was slowing, and all that remained was a wet drizzle. As Jones moved off, the phone began to ring, reverberating through the car.

"I wonder who that is?" said Jones. "Shall I ignore it?"

"Answer it," said Autumn, somewhat quietly.

Jones pushed the button on her steering wheel. "Hello, this is Jones."

"Jones, hello," said a man's voice. "This is Drew Anderson."

"Hello Drew," said Jones, raising her eyebrows towards Autumn. "How are you? How is Iris?"

"No change I'm afraid," he said.

"I'm so sorry to hear that. How can I help you?"

"I just wanted to let you know-" Drew took in a deep breath. It sounded like he was trying to suck in a cry. "I just wanted to let you know, ah, we've decided to postpone the wedding."

"Oh no," Jones said, genuinely sad for them both.

"It just makes sense," he said. "A mess, but it must be done. So I just wanted you to know that there was no rush about the Memory Box."

"Sure, thank you for thinking of me," said Jones. "Do you want me to hold on to it, or shall I return it to you for now?"

"Gosh, I can't think straight at the moment," said Drew. "Perhaps if you gave my mother a call. She's kind of taking over sorting out the wedding stuff. She'll know what to do. You have her number?"

"Yes I do," said Jones. "Not a problem. I'll give her a call this afternoon. And Drew, if there is anything you need, anything at all, please just let me know."

"Thank you, Jones. I'd better go."

"Bye Drew," and Jones ended the call.

"How sad," said Autumn.

"Very," said Jones. "I'm sure the wedding will go ahead but what a palaver it will be changing everything."

"I wouldn't be so sure," said Autumn. "It doesn't sound like Iris is getting any better. What if they can't save her?"

Jones shook her head sadly as she pulled up in front of The Memory Bank.

"Is this close enough?" asked Jones. "Can I do anything?"

"This is perfect," said Autumn. "I can feel the energy already. I'm fine. You go home and I'll see you in the morning."

"Oh I wish there was a way we could communicate with each other when I'm at home," said Jones. "I know I'm going to panic all night."

"Look, Jones!" Autumn was waving her arm in front of her sister's face. "Look, I'm getting stronger already. You can see it. I'll be fine!"

Autumn was right, the colours in her arm were looking decidedly brighter. Jones relaxed a little.

"OK," said Jones. "As long as you're sure. I am rather exhausted. I just want to go home and have a hot show and a quick tea before bed."

"Off you go Jones," said Autumn. "You're not going to get rid of me that easily!" With that Autumn ascended out of the car and waved at Jones before floating through The Memory Bank's front door.

CHAPTER 14

The next morning when Jones heard the rain thrumming on the iron roof, she decided to trial Sybil's drive-through service.

"Of course," said Sybil. "I'm parked in the same spot as yesterday. I'll see you soon."

Jones had also added an egg and bacon sandwich to her order and was very much looking forward to it as she slipped on a pair of jeans and a navy hoodie with *'Sometimes the impossible just takes a little bit longer'* from Ghost Whisperer printed across the front. Jones had had it custom-made a few weeks ago, and today was the first time she would wear it. She wanted to create something that was a nod to her sister, without appearing too bizarre to the general public, or too insensitive to Autumn. This Melinda Gordon quote struck a chord.

As Jones jumped into her Mini Cooper and drove towards Sybil's, she again found herself wondering how much longer the impossible would last. She was still worried about Autumn. Although Jones was confident her sister would still be waiting for her at The Memory Bank this morning, how long would it last? And how much did these low-energy moments impact her? Did Jones or The Memory Bank only have a finite amount of energy available to her, and when it ran out, would that be the end? Jones would have preferred not to think about it at all, but she knew, realistically, that one day her sister would truly be gone forever. What would she do then?

They still had no idea why exactly Autumn was here. At first, Jones had been sure her sister would leave once the mystery of her death was solved. But now that Jamie Royce, Autumn's ex-boyfriend, was sitting in a jail cell waiting for his court appearance, Autumn was still here. Jones had also considered that Autumn remained on earth to help her reestablish The Memory Bank, and if that were the case, then it was reasonable to assume that Autumn wouldn't be here for much longer. Was last night's scare showing the truth of this?

Fortunately, Jones had pulled up alongside Sybil's coffee van, so she turned her mind to breakfast.

"Thank you, Sybil!" Jones walked the few steps from her car to the van grateful for a slight lull in the downpour. "I could get used to this!"

Sybil smiled at her. Today she had her grey hair in two long braids over her shoulders. She wore bright red glasses, and a knitted poncho covered in gum leaves.

"A pleasure as always!" said Sybil. "Have you heard anything more about Iris?"

"Drew told me yesterday there was no change," Jones replied, taking a welcome sip of her hot flat white. "I'm going to be ringing his mother this morning, so maybe she'll know more."

"Ah, the lovely Davina," said Sybil.

"You know her?" asked Jones. "I've only met her once."

"We went to school together," said Sybil. "She's a nice enough person, but someone who certainly goes after what she wants."

Jones wanted to ask more, but her car was idling, and more people had arrived. She waved thanks to Sybil and headed towards The Memory Bank.

Jones was glad she had driven in today. She was anticipating having to take the Memory Box to Drew's mother, Davina, but it served a secondary purpose of getting her to The Memory Bank as quickly as possible this morning.

"Autumn!" Jones called before she had even fully opened the front door. "Autumn! Are you here?"

It flashed across her mind that if someone was walking past The Memory Bank just as she was calling out to Autumn, they would think she was having a breakdown. Jones realised she needed to be more careful. Just because Autumn's presence was normal to her now, didn't mean she could rest on her laurels. No one else knew about Autumn, and she knew she needed to keep it that way.

"I'm here Jones! I'm fine!" And she was, perched in one of her preferred locations, on the circular counter in the middle of the store. The lights and the chandelier came to life, and Jones exhaled a breath she hadn't realised she was holding.

"Thank goodness," said Jones. "How are you feeling? Any ill effects from yesterday?"

"Completely back to normal I think," said Autumn, taking a look at her arms and her body. Jones agreed, she did look back to her normal self. Her normal ghost self at least.

"Well that is a relief," said Jones. "Now I can focus on my day. What time is it?"

"Only just after eight," said Autumn. "You've got enough time to sit down, enjoy your breakfast, and take a breather."

Autumn was right. Jones had barely stopped moving since she

woke up, anxious to get to The Memory Bank as soon as possible. She sat down, with her coffee and sandwich, at one of the customer tables near the side windows. For the first time in a while, Jones reflected on the past few weeks. Since they'd solved Autumn's murder, things had started to get into a bit of a flow. Most mornings Jones opened up The Memory Bank at nine, although Atlas had been taking the Saturday morning shift most weeks, and the occasional additional weekday shift if Jones needed him.

One day a few weeks ago she had travelled to Adelaide to take a few things from her cottage and get it prepared to be listed for rent. Jones had decided to rent it out for short-term accommodation. That way she could access it whenever she needed to, but it would be used, and as a bonus, she would have a side income stream coming in. Although The Memory Bank was going well, Jones realised the regular journalism income she was used to was very different to the varying sales she made now. Although there was money available to her from her father's and now her sister's estates, she was trying to save that, and only dipped into some of it for the renovations of The Memory Bank. Jones wanted to live on the income she had coming in from The Memory Bank whilst also trying to restock and keep the store fresh. She had realised more income streams were needed and the cottage rental was the first one to come to fruition. Other ideas had been swirling through her mind. After working on Iris and Drew's Memory Box, she realised this, and other opportunities were open to her, especially if she started thinking of ways to apply her journalism skills.

"I'd better call Davina before I open up," said Jones to, she presumed, Autumn although she couldn't currently see her.

"Good plan!" Autumn's voice came from a distance.

"Where are you?" Jones called.

"I'm in the secret room!" said Autumn. The secret room was a little hideout neither of them had known about before Autumn's death. With her newfound ability to walk through walls, Autumn had discovered it a few weeks ago, and Jones had even spent a night sleeping on the sofa inside. They had since pushed the bookshelf back in front of the door, keeping it hidden. Neither of them knew what they were going to do with it, but for some reason, they had both decided to keep it between themselves. Not even Atlas knew about it.

Autumn floated through one of the rear walls and over to Jones. "I call it my escape room," said Autumn.

"Well, I get the irony. There's no way you can't escape it!" Jones smiled.

"Ha ha," said Autumn. "No, I call it my escape room because it's a room that I can escape to, only I can get in."

"That does sound nice," said Jones. She realised she had no true understanding of what Autumn's life was like now. As a ghost, she could go anywhere she liked, and no one was the wiser. Yet it also meant people could always come into Autumn's space and she had no control over this. Except for the escape room.

Jones picked up her phone and searched for Davina's number before dialling. She tilted her head and looked at Autumn as she waited for someone to pick up.

"Hello, this is Davina," a strong female voice came through the earpiece.

"Hello Davina, this is Jones Eldershaw, from The Memory Bank."

"Hello dear, how can I help you?"

"I spoke with Drew yesterday. He told me he'd decided to postpone the wedding."

"Yes, it's the best thing to do," Davina said, no real emotion coming through her voice.

"Yes, I suppose so," said Jones. "It is a tricky one."

"A little tricky, but we'll get it sorted. Harris is helping me make all the phone calls."

"That's good to hear. I'm calling because Drew wasn't sure what to do about the Memory Box I've been putting together. As it's full of personal items, I wasn't sure if I should keep it here in the Bank, or if I should return it to someone?"

"Good point dear," said Davina. "Let me think. What would be the best thing?" Davina paused for a moment before continuing. "Look, I do feel it would be better if I looked after it, for the family. At least for now. Everything is inside?"

"Yes," said Jones. "Except for the Memory Book that I haven't finished yet, and also I returned Charlie's items to him yesterday"

"Oh, you did?" Davina seemed surprised at this.

"He asked me to," said Jones. "I suppose he'll add it back in before the wedding when you know the new date." If there is a wedding, thought Jones.

"Yes, of course," said Davina. "Will you be putting the Memory Book on hold for now? Seeing as we don't know what is going on with

Iris, things might change."

"You're probably right," said Jones. "I'll keep the notes here with me, and I can restart whenever Drew and Iris think it is appropriate."

"Good," said Davina. "Now, we're meeting at the winery for lunch today, just the family. Do you think you could drop past with the Memory Box around one o'clock? You're welcome to stay for some lunch if you like."

"I can make that work," said Jones. "And lunch does sound good. Will you be in the main restaurant?"

"Yes, yes," said Davina. "The winery is closed today. It's just the family. Harris is cooking. Not Drew of course. He's at the hospital with Iris. But we're going to have a bit of a meeting to get everything organised."

"Yes, I understand. Well, I'll see you then," said Jones. She hung up and looked at Autumn. "The family is meeting for lunch today, and I'm invited."

"Oh, that will be the perfect opportunity to investigate!" said Autumn, clutching her hands together. "And I'll do some snooping around. It is the site of Iris's last meal before she collapsed."

"Indeed," said Jones. "The most likely place she was poisoned." She looked up at Autumn, apprehension on her face. "Perhaps lunch wasn't the best idea?"

"Oh gosh, you're right!" said Autumn. "Maybe just pretend you've already eaten. Although will that look suspicious?"

"I think I'm just going to have to wing it when I get there," said Jones. "But I'm sorry Autumn, there is no way I can allow you to go with me today. It's just too risky."

Autumn pouted. "Allow me! I don't think that's how this whole thing works," she replied to her sister.

"You can't seriously think it's a good idea," said Jones. "Not after yesterday. Please, no. Look, I'll make sure I use this time to ask as many questions as I can. And, surely the police have already been to check out the kitchen. I don't think you'll find a bottle marked 'Poison' sitting on the counter."

Autumn rolled her eyes and sighed before zooming into the air and flying in circles around the chandelier. "You're right, you're right. I know. But ugh! I just wanted to get out and about. It's so frustrating that it seems I'm permanently connected to the Bank!"

Jones stared at her sister, not expecting such an outburst. "Autumn, are you ok?" she asked, head tilted up, watching her sister who was now doing figure eights around two of the hanging light bulbs.

"I think the novelty of this whole ghost thing has well and truly worn off," said Autumn. "We have no idea why I'm still here, and my life as I knew it has vanished. You're the only person I've spoken to in months, and honestly, I'm starting to go a little stir-crazy. I know there isn't a thing you can do, and I understand you're worried about me, but sometimes I just don't know how much longer I can stand this!"

Without realising, Jones had tears running down her cheeks. She started sobbing, and the cries came in the form of gulps. It was as though all the tension and emotion she had been holding since Autumn reappeared was finally releasing. She dropped her head, and just let the tears and sobs come. She'd lost her sister once, and now it seemed inevitable she would lose her sister again.

"Jones, what's wrong?" the worried voice of Atlas echoed through The Memory Bank. Neither Jones nor Autumn had noticed him unlocking the door.

Hastily, Jones shook her hands and attempted to wipe the tears from her cheeks. She realised that was completely inadequate, and turned to face Atlas in all her blotchy glory.

"Oh Atlas, I'm fine," she said. "I just seem to be having a bad morning."

"What's happened? Are you ok?" Atlas dumped his laptop bag and the carrier of two coffees he always seemed to know to arrive with, and walked to Jones, clearly not knowing whether to take her hands or hug her. It wasn't quite the relationship they had, so instead he patted her on the arm.

"Nothing really," said Jones. She glanced up at Autumn and saw her gliding away towards her escape room. "I think with Iris in the hospital, and the shock of that, it's just brought up a lot about Autumn and her death. I'm ok. I just needed to let things out I think."

"Do you want to perhaps go home, and have the day off?" Atlas suggested.

Jones looked at him and smiled. She didn't know what she would have done without him over the last few months. When she needed a physical person to pick up her slack, Atlas always seemed to be there, ready and willing.

"Thanks, Atlas," said Jones. "But I'll be fine. Thanks for letting me get emotional. I'll be back to normal in a moment. I'll just go and get myself sorted."

Jones made her way to the bathroom. It was lined with heritage green subway tiles, and black and white penny tiles on the floor. The toilet cubicle was dark wood, and this, along with the white pedestal basin was all original. They hadn't touched it during renovations, but Jones had added some fluffy towels, a few pot plants, and of course, candles, to dress up the room.

Now she leant her hands on the basin and stared at herself in the mirror. She took a few deep breaths and, ignoring the mascara that was now blurred down her cheeks, tried to make sense of Autumn's blowup. Maybe being here wasn't right. Maybe Autumn should be allowed to 'go into the light' as they say. Was Jones being selfish by relying so much on Autumn? But if it was in her power to release Autumn, then what exactly was she supposed to do? Autumn's presence was a complete mystery. Yet the idea of never seeing her sister again made her heart race and a wave of sadness came over her.

"Pull yourself together Jones," she said. "You know this isn't forever, so make the most of the time you've got. And honestly, you're the only one that can steer this ship, so get out there and get going!"

Jones rolled her eyes at her attempt at a pep talk. She took one of the towels, dampening a corner, and attempted to wipe away the mascara. It left her cheeks red and a little sore, but most of the mascara was gone. She could pass for having gotten caught in a downpour which, in this unusual November weather, was entirely possible.

"You've got this!" Jones said to herself in the mirror. Rolling her shoulders back, she swung the door open and strode out into The Memory Bank.

CHAPTER 15

Jones hadn't seen Autumn since her morning outburst. It made her ill to think Autumn was upset with her and questioning whether she even wanted to be here. The only upside was that Jones was able to leave The Memory Bank without Autumn begging to come along. Jones knew she would only panic the whole time she was at Casa Galati if Autumn had joined her.

Whizzing down Main Street in her Mini, Jones continued out of the town for a few kilometres before turning down a dirt road. A brown sign pointed towards Casa Galati, a bunch of grapes to the right of the name indicating it was a winery tourist location. The dirt road wound up through paddocks of sheep or cattle on one side, and vines on the other. The yellow wattle and pink gum blossoms coloured the path, and as she indicated to turn into the winery, for the first time in a while, the sun came out.

The white dirt driveway was lined with tall pencil conifers, while the cellar door and restaurant at the top were framed by two very old manna gums towering above. As expected, the car park was almost empty, except for a couple of four-wheel drives, a ute, and a white Land Rover. Jones pulled her Mini in front of the rammed earth wall of the cellar door. Getting out of the car, to her left she saw the dark grey walls and large windows of the restaurant. Jones could see that all the chairs were up on the tables, except for one.

"Knock, knock!" Jones called as she pushed the restaurant's door open.

She could hear voices at the far end of the room where there were swinging kitchen doors. Walking across the polished concrete floors, Jones called out again. "Hello!" Three heads turned her way. Drew's brother Harris sat with his parents, each of them with a glass of red in front of them.

"Jones!" Davina's voice boomed across the room. "Come, sit down. So good you could make it."

"Thank you," said Jones. "I've left the Memory Box in my boot. It's a bit heavy, so thought it best we transfer it later."

"Of course, of course," said Davina. "Let's have lunch first. Sit down." Mr Anderson stood and came around to pull out a seat for Jones.

"Thank you," she said, a little surprised at the formality, and took her seat.

"You remember my husband, Douglas," said Davina. "And my youngest son Harris." Both men nodded hello.

"Yes, hello," said Jones, not sure what else to say to the mute pair.

"Let's get lunch started shall we Harris," said Davina.

"Sure, sure," said Harris. He ran his hands through his hair, before rising from the table to show his white chef's uniform and striped apron. "It won't be long," he said, making his way into the kitchen.

"Ignore this mopey bunch," said Davina. "We're all just feeling a little exhausted after the last few days, and who knew how much there was to do just to postpone a wedding!" She let out a bit of a laugh, before shaking her head and taking a sip of the red wine in front of her. "Help yourself, Jones." Davina's head nod indicated the bottle of wine in the middle of the table.

Jones didn't hesitate. Although she was only planning to have a glass, the Casa Galati wine was renowned, and she imagined the Andersons were having one of the better bottles of red. She poured a moderate glass and took a sniff before sipping. As she expected, it was delicious.

"Tara does an excellent job," said Davina, taking another sip herself. "Her father must be very proud."

Jones recalled that not only was Tara Galati now the head winemaker at Casa Galati, but she was also Drew's ex-girlfriend. The proximity to Iris's last meal didn't escape Jones. Yet she sat at the table with people who were also in attendance at that lunch, along with Harris and Drew. Any one of them could have slipped something into Iris's food. Thankfully the wine bottle was already opened and being consumed by three of the four possible suspects in attendance, so Jones felt more comfortable about drinking that. Lunch may be another matter.

"It is a *very* nice wine," said Jones. "I suppose you come here a lot?'

Davina nodded. "Yes. I mean we always loved the winery and used to come a lot when Drew and Tara, well, when they were a couple. Now that Harris is the head chef here, of course, we love to support him. He's doing so well. I'm told the kitchen has been transformed since he arrived. But you'll see. Harris is a great cook."

At that moment, Harris came out carrying two large bowls, and following behind him was a tall, stunning woman, with plates and cutlery.

"Oh Tara," exclaimed Davina. "That's not your job!"

"Don't be silly Davina," said Tara. "It's family today. Of course, I can carry the plates."

"Family?" thought Jones. Does Tara consider herself family, or was she just referring to the Anderson's themselves?

"Oh, hello." Tara smiled in Jones's direction.

"Tara, this is Jones, the lady I was telling you about," said Davina.

"Yes, Jones from The Memory Bank," said Tara. "I used to see your sister a bit. She was lovely. So sad what happened." Jones smiled and nodded her head. She didn't recall Autumn saying she knew Tara particularly well. She would have to check with her.

"Yes," said Jones. "I've been working on something special for Drew and Iris. Here's hoping it can be revealed soon."

"We've told Tara all about it," said Davina. "Of course, the wedding was going to be here at the winery, so Tara's had a lot of involvement in getting everything arranged. Done a wonderful job, as always. Pity it isn't going ahead."

Jones wrinkled her forehead for a moment. Surely Davina had misspoken. Not going ahead, *for now*.

"Everything is fine, Davina," said Tara. "We'll get it all sorted. Don't worry about a thing. Now," Tara leant over and picked up the empty wine bottle. "I'll just go grab another one of these. Enjoy your lunch!"

"You're not joining us, Tara?" said Davina.

"No, I've got a few things to do out the back," she said. "A bit of a hiccup with the deliveries, so I'll go and get that sorted. But not before I grab you that wine."

Tara strode off in the direction of a small bar that was in the corner of the room. Reaching high in one of the racks, obviously where the best wine was kept, she pulled down a bottle, and with the expertise of a sommelier, uncorked the wine and poured herself a small glass to taste. "Perfect," she said quietly, before bringing the bottle over to the table.

"Thank you, Tara," said Davina. Tara poured them all a glass, before leaving the bottle with them and making her way back to the kitchen.

"Gnocchi and salad today," said Harris. "Help yourselves!"

Jones looked around as everyone stared at her. "Guests first," said Davina.

Picking up the spoon, Jones hesitated before scooping up her serving. She realised a communal meal was unlikely to be poisoned.

The gnocchi smelt beautiful. "Pumpkin with burnt butter and sage," Harris explained as Jones finished. "And a blistered tomato salad with arugula and a balsamic dressing."

"You're not allergic to anything, are you Jones?" asked Davina.

"No, not at all," said Jones. "It all looks delicious, thank you."

"There are some wild herbs in there too," explained Harris. "I love foraging. Most people have no idea what's all around them."

"Really?" asked Jones. "You can find wild herbs around here?"

"Absolutely! And not just herbs. All sorts of things. Berries, fungi, root vegetables, and all sorts of greens."

"And you use a lot of that here, at the winery?"

"Some I do," said Harris. "A lot I just experiment with. I enjoy heading out and seeing what I can find."

"Speaking of heading out," said Davina. "Are you off to that mushroom tour again tonight?"

"Sure am," replied Harris, nodding and placing a forkful of salad in his mouth.

"Oh, is that the ghost mushrooms everyone is talking about?" asked Jones.

"Yes," said Harris. "They're amazing. You really should take a look. I think there are only three nights left. Last night is Saturday I believe." Harris smiled at Jones and took another sip of wine.

Everyone was silent whilst they filled their plates and began to eat. It truly was delicious. Harris was a very good chef, even when it came to whipping up a quick meal for his family.

"Have you heard how Iris is this morning," asked Jones, wiping balsamic from the corner of her mouth.

"No, nothing," said Davina. "What about you Harris? Have you heard from Drew?"

"Nope, not at all," he replied shaking his head before eating a large mouthful of gnocchi.

"I guess that means there's no change. So sad," said Davina. "Can't imagine who would want to hurt her. She always seemed like such a delicate thing."

"She wasn't delicate, Mum," said Harris. "I think she did half the work on that farm. She was always the one running all over the place, getting the cattle on and off that truck of theirs. Charlie never leaves the farm. I don't know what he's going to do whilst she isn't there to keep things moving."

Jones was surprised to hear all of this about Iris. She realised despite all the interviews she'd done, most people had spoken about Iris as a younger person when she had her cancer, and how amazing it was for her to pull through. No one seemed to talk much about how much she did on the farm with Charlie.

"So, Iris and Charlie run the farm together, is that right?" Jones asked.

"Yes dear," said Douglas, speaking for the first time. "And from all accounts I've heard they both do a splendid job. Charlie sure knows his stuff and he's really brought on the pasture over there. The two of them have a good setup."

"Well of course they do," said Davina. "They've both been handed prime land, and no doubt have expansion plans."

"Mum!" said Harris. "Just because you managed to take over Dad's family farm when you married him, doesn't mean Iris has the same plans. You've got to stop worrying."

Jones looked at Harris, her confusion clear, because he went on to explain. "When Mum married Dad, she somehow managed to get all his family's land incorporated into the Wattle Farms estate, making this huge parcel. And now Mum thinks just because she was wily enough to do it, that Iris is planning the same thing."

"Shoosh, Harris," said Davina. "The poor girl is in hospital. Speak nicely, please." Jones looked at Davina, who was frowning at her lunch. Jones wasn't quite sure if it was because Harris was speaking inappropriately, or because he had hit the nail on the head.

"So Iris is going to stay working on the farm with Charlie? Is that the plan after the wedding?" asked Jones. She hoped her digging didn't sound obvious, and just innocent curiosity, because at the moment this hostility seemed like a prime motive for attempted murder.

"Yes," said Davina. "I believe everything was going to continue just the way it was. Drew and his father running Wattle Farms, and Iris and Charlie running Twelve Oaks. Of course, there was a bit to nut out due to them getting married, but that wasn't going to be a problem, was it Douglas?"

"No," said Douglas. "At least not from what our lawyers said. Fairly straightforward apparently."

"Yes, with only one son on the farm," said Davina. "It sure makes things easier." Jones looked between Davina and Harris. Based on Davina's tone of voice and her glance at Harris, Jones suspected it wasn't making things easier at all.

"Ugh, Mum," said Harris, standing abruptly. "Couldn't help but have a dig." He grabbed his wine glass and plate and walked into the kitchen.

"Ignore him, Jones," said Davina. "Harris gets a bit jealous at times. Thinks he can have his cake and eat it too. But unfortunately, that's not the way family farms work."

Jones nodded and took another mouthful of the tomato and arugula salad. Glancing up she saw Douglas watching her before he smiled and resumed eating.

"I suppose there is quite a list of things to do for the wedding," said Jones, attempting to get Davina talking again.

"Is there!" said Davina. "Iris said it was a simple wedding, but boy oh boy are there a lot of people involved."

But Davina was cut short by the sound of shouting coming from the kitchen and the loudest of the voices was Tara's.

CHAPTER 16

"I can't believe I'm surrounded by idiots!" they heard her yell before Harris responded.

"Look, I'm sorry," said Harris. "But there's nothing I can do about it."

"First I have to organise this wedding, now I have to cancel everyone, and you're telling me I'm going to have to accept a huge order of pork for a wedding that isn't even happening!"

Jones glanced at Davina and Douglas. Douglas showed no expression and just continued eating the food on his plate. Davina on the other hand had her head turned to the shouting, her face a look of fury.

"You'd better get it sorted or it's coming out of your pay cheque!" The next thing they heard was a door slam and then silence.

"Very sorry you had to hear that," said Davina. "Tara is a lovely girl but we've put her under a bit of stress. And of course, I doubt Harris is very easy to work with."

"Oh, is that what you think is it!" said Harris, who had appeared by the table. "No wonder you didn't want me on the farm. I wouldn't bend to your will like Drew does. All these women around me who think they can just tell me what to do. I need a restaurant of my own, and soon!"

"Harris!" said Davina. "That is enough! We can talk about this later."

"I don't have anything to talk about," said Harris. He grabbed the red wine bottle, poured what was left into his glass, and stormed out the front door of the restaurant.

"Sorry Jones," said Davina. "I think we're all just a little bit on edge. It's been a tough few days."

"Of course," said Jones. "I'll get out of your hair. Douglas, do you think perhaps you could help me with the Memory Box? Then I can leave you all to it."

"Yes absolutely," said Douglas, rising from his chair. "Lead the way."

Jones stood, wiping her fingers on a napkin and placing it on her plate.

"It was a lovely lunch," she said. "Harris is an excellent cook."

"Thank you dear," said Davina. "He certainly has that going for him."

Jones said her goodbyes to Davina and walked out to her car, Douglas following behind.

"Families can be tough sometimes," said Douglas quietly as Jones opened her boot.

Jones nodded. "They certainly can," she said. "But I'm sure it will all work out."

"Yes, one way or another," said Douglas, lifting the Memory Box from the boot. "Jeepers, this *is* a bit heavy."

Jones laughed. "It is. Thank you for grabbing it. You can see why I left it in the car."

"Well, thank you for bringing it all the way out here," said Douglas. "Hopefully you can visit the winery again sometime in less, ah, dramatic circumstances." He smiled, nodded, and then walked away.

Jones jumped in her car, her mind racing. She had learnt so much, more than she expected. Plus she got an amazing free lunch. Jones couldn't wait to get back to Autumn and tell her everything.

Whizzing through the back roads of Lilly Pilly Creek, Jones thought over everything she had heard. It seemed there were a few people with motives for murder, and a temper to go with it. Set against the backdrop of a stunning winery and delicious food, well, there was a lot to consider.

Jones was glad when she finally pulled up in front of The Memory Bank but frowned when she saw numerous cars parked out the front. She knew it was ridiculous to be disappointed that there were customers in The Memory Bank however, she was hoping for a quiet moment with Autumn. Then she remembered. Autumn may not even be there waiting for her. She was most likely still holed up in her escape room after her outburst. Jones was overcome with sadness, and for a moment she remained in her car, not wanting to face whatever was waiting for her.

As a ghost, Autumn was in between two worlds. The second world neither of them knew anything about. They were just doing their best to manage the current situation. A situation they could never have imagined in their wildest dreams. However, Jones realised she hadn't truly taken the time to consider it from Autumn's point of view. To Jones it seemed like Autumn was just gliding around in the world, having great fun, no responsibilities, and the ability to walk through walls. It was Jones that was doing the heavy lifting, both literally and figuratively. Jones was the one with the responsibility to ensure The Memory Bank was serving its customers to the best of its ability. Jones was the one that had to talk with all the customers, order the stock, manage the lockboxes, and ensure the Bank was making a profit. Yet it wasn't until today Jones realised that Autumn would quite like to be doing all of that too. Plus, drinking gin at Hugo's bar, having a conversation with Wren about which girl she was going on a date with that weekend, pruning their Mum's rose in the back garden, and, of course, planning for the future. Autumn, as it seemed to them, had no future. No future except either to be in this world, invisible to everyone except Jones, with no real ability to interact with it, or to no longer be in this world, to move into another plane they couldn't possibly imagine.

Jones rested her head on the steering wheel for a moment, overwhelmed with all the mistakes she had made and the complete lack of consideration she had given to Autumn. If Autumn was still inside The Memory Bank, and gosh she desperately hoped she was, Jones was going to talk to Autumn, listen to how she was feeling, and do her absolute best to make her existence as a ghost as happy as possible. Because Jones simply did not want to think about the prospect of losing Autumn again.

"Come on Jones," she thought. "You can't hide out here forever." Jones grabbed her handbag, closed and locked the car door, and headed inside.

She was pleased to see a few customers dotted throughout the main area. Atlas was perched up at the counter, laptop to hand but ready to assist any customer who needed it.

"How's the new office going?" asked Jones as she walked up.

Atlas's head shot up with a grin. "Oh, it's going to be amazing! Come look." Atlas bounced off his stool and Jones followed him to the glass room that had, in a matter of hours, become Atlas's new headquarters.

"I hope this is ok?" Atlas was pointing to a sign he had stuck on the glass door.

"Wayfinder Labs by Atlas Hemming," read Jones. "I love it!" The logo was a clever mix of a globe, a compass, and what appeared to be a representation of the internet, and Jones had to admit she was impressed.

"Thanks, Jones," said Atlas. "I even have a client meeting me here later today. I'd never have been able to do that from my bedroom in my parent's house!"

"That is great Atlas," said Jones. "I'm so pleased. It works well for both of us, so thanks for suggesting it." She smiled at him. It was going to be nice to have another person in The Memory Bank with her.

"How did it go at the winery?" Jones quickly turned her head to see Autumn floating to her left, smiling.

Jones tilted her head towards Atlas, indicating she had to move somewhere else before they spoke.

"I'll leave you to it," she said to Atlas. "I'm back so I'll manage the Bank customers."

Walking past the central counter and towards a row of

bookshelves, Jones had to admit she was shaking. The relief that Autumn had come to her, smiling, was more overwhelming than Jones had been expecting. She realised she had been imagining the worst.

"So, tell me everything!" said Autumn, hovering close to her sister.

Jones quickly glanced around before starting the story. She told Autumn everything, emphasising the matriarch status of Davina, the black sheep reputation of Harris, and his outburst at both his mother and Tara.

"So, Harris certainly has a motive to ruin Drew's life," said Autumn.

"Not to mention Davina," said Jones. "She's the one pulling the strings in that family, and I don't think she was all that impressed that Iris was marrying Drew."

"You would have thought it was a perfect match," said Autumn. "Two established farming families coming together."

"Not exactly how Davina sees it," said Jones.

"And you met the ex-girlfriend?" asked Autumn.

"Yes," said Jones. "She seems quite nice. Although I think she has a bit of a temper. She and Harris were having an argument in the kitchen just before I left. I think Harris had made a mistake with an order."

"Stressed from the fall out of poisoning her rival, perhaps?" Autumn smiled and Jones shrugged.

"She did mention she knew you."

"Really?" said Autumn. "Possibly we crossed paths once or twice, but I don't think I ever spoke to her. I think the winery sponsored a lot of events and donated wine, so maybe it was something to do with that."

"Well, I don't really think she has anything to do with it," said Jones. "But Harris, and by extension, his mother are looking like rather prime suspects. Plus, Harris cooked the food when Iris was there, so how easy would it have been to slip Iris the poison?"

"Easy?" said Autumn. "Or too easy?"

"Now you are starting to sound like a detective," Jones laughed as her phone rang.

"Are you ready for a drink?" asked Wren. "I'm ready for a drink!"

"One of those days was it Wren?" Jones said, making her way out of the stacks.

"Just a lot of tricky customers today," she said, a little dramatically. "I can't tell you a thing, but we can at least share a wine. Ready?"

Jones glanced at her watch and saw it was still only just four o'clock. "It's still a bit early Wren. I left Atlas here whilst I had lunch with the Andersons, so I need to stay until closing. Meet you there as soon as I'm done?"

"I suppose I can wait another hour," said Wren. "I can of course find something to do. I'll meet you there, no later than five oh five."

Jones laughed. "It's a date!"

CHAPTER 17

Jones was true to her word. She found Wren leaning against the door frame of Hugo's, looking like a model for Business Chic Monthly in a tweed skirt and blazer, both highlighted with silver buttons, and a white silk blouse. Tall nude pumps finished the outfit.

"A particularly bad day?" Jones asked walking up.

Wren stood and pulled open the door. "You have no idea!"

Jones and Wren walked directly to the bar, with Autumn floating ahead, and surprisingly for Jones, perching herself on the bench behind Hugo.

Jones was intrigued to see Tara at the bar, sharing a glass of her own wine with Hugo. Hugo smiled when he saw them, and Jones nodded at Tara, acknowledging their meeting earlier that day.

"What can I get for you, ladies?" he asked as they sat down. Jones felt her stomach flip hearing his voice. His tousled hair, stubble and check shirt did seem to affect her. Autumn was grinning, so Jones wasn't hiding her feelings as well as she would have liked.

"Wine," said Wren. "A lot of wine!"

Hugo pointed at Tara and said "Well, may I suggest a bottle of Tara's red? I've just tried the latest vintage and it is delicious!"

"Sounds perfect," said Wren. "I do love a bottle of Galati," and she smiled at Tara.

Tara returned the smile and, picking up her bottle and glass, replied "Enjoy!" before moving over to an empty booth and taking a seat.

Jones didn't know Tara at all well, but the enthusiasm for her own wine somehow seemed forced. She knew Tara had had a tough day, or afternoon at least, so that was surely understandable. And Jones couldn't help glancing between Tara and Hugo, wondering if there was a stronger connection than just the wine.

Jones shook her head and looked up as Hugo popped the cork on a bottle of the Galati Sangiovese and poured an extra large glass for Wren. "Here you go!" Wren couldn't help but laugh when she saw the pour of red. Jones laughed along whilst Hugo poured her a more respectable-sized glass.

"Thanks, Hugo," Jones smiled. "Thanks, Hugo," Autumn mimicked, winking at her sister.

Jones sent her sister an eye-roll when Hugo had moved off to serve another customer, taking a sip of Tara's wine.

"Gee," said Jones. "This is delicious. It's different to what I drank today, but still very nice."

"Oh, did you get one of the good bottles today?" asked Wren, clearly jealous.

"I *was* invited to a *private luncheon,*" Jones said, putting on a false posh accent.

"Lucky you!" said Wren. "And what was it like? What's the word with Iris?"

"They know nothing more about her condition," said Jones. "But they are postponing the wedding."

Wren nodded, indicating she already knew this.

"Are the Andersons the reason why you've had a tough day?"

asked Jones, raising an eyebrow.

"Let's just say, it has something to do with it," said Wren. "But I can't say any more."

Jones knew there was something there, possibly information that would be very pertinent to their 'case' but had to respect Wren's very professional legal boundaries.

"Hmmm," said Jones. "Well, it's put Tara in a bit of a pickle because I think most of the 'un-organising' falls to her." Jones leaned in closer to Wren. "She wasn't very happy about it this afternoon."

Jones jumped a little when she saw someone sit down next to Wren. Prue Timberley. Some may call her Jones's nemesis. Prue had caused Jones a lot of angst in the week after reopening The Memory Bank. Not only was Jones just learning the ropes at The Bank, but she was also trying to identify her sister's murderer. It was Prue who threw a complete spanner in the works by trying, rather underhandedly, to take The Memory Bank out from under her. Fortunately, Prue had failed, but Jones had barely shared a passing glance with Prue since. It appeared that was about to change.

Prue leaned completely across Wren and whispered, "Jones!" Jones looked at Prue, a quizzical expression on her face. "I thought you might like to know," she almost hissed in her attempt to whisper. "Charlie Wainwright has just been taken to hospital."

"What?" Jones said, a lot louder than Prue. Autumn was now hovering right across from Prue, taking in every word she said.

"Shhh," Prue said. "I shouldn't be telling you this. But I know you were there when Iris collapsed and well," Prue looked around to ensure no one else was listening. "Don't you think it's a little suspicious?"

She did indeed. Jones nodded at Prue, and they shared a meaningful glance. Jones was very surprised that Prue had decided to impart this information to her. It wasn't as though Prue, or anyone for that matter, had any idea that she, with Autumn's help, was currently investigating Iris's poisoning. Had Jones gained some sort of reputation in the past few weeks that she wasn't aware of? Since she had been the one to solve the mystery of Autumn's murder.

"It seems to me," said Prue. "And I'm not an investigator, but it would seem that someone has something against the Wainwright family." Prue raised her eyebrows at Jones, and then turned to signal Hugo. She asked Hugo for a wine glass and moved over to join Tara and her bottle of wine, without saying another word.

"My goodness," said Jones. "I can't believe it."

"I know," said Wren. "It does seem like someone has it out for the Wainwrights. And one family seems to have the strongest connection." Wren did genuinely look worried. Jones knew Wren had a connection to the Andersons through her work, but what this meant for her, Jones had no idea.

"How do you think Prue found out about it?" asked Jones.

"Prue has many connections in this town," said Wren. "I'm thinking she just happened to be in the right place at the right time to catch this bit of gossip. It was interesting that she decided to impart this information to you though."

"I know!" said Jones. "Honestly, I do not understand that

woman."

"Look who's just walked in," Autumn said.

Jones turned to the open door of Hugo's and saw Sergeant Christopher Schmidt standing there.

CHAPTER 18

"Christopher," said Jones quietly. Wren caught it and turned.

"Sergeant Schmidt in the bar?" said Wren. "And in casual clothes!"

Christopher caught Jones's eye, smiled, and walked over.

"Hi Jones, Wren," he nodded.

"Sergeant Schmidt," said Wren.

"Hi Christopher," said Jones. "I thought you might be, ah, busy." Hastily she took a sip of her wine, realising her mistake and hoping Wren would cover for her.

"Did you want a glass?" Wren asked, pointing at their bottle of red.

"Oh," said Christopher. "Actually, that would be nice. If you don't mind?"

"Not at all," said Wren. "Were you meeting anyone?"

Jones nearly scoffed with a mouthful of wine, surprised at the questioning Wren easily offered up to the local police Sergeant.

"No," he nodded pulling up a stool. "Just thought I'd come in for a glass tonight. Haven't been in here much. It's pretty popular," he said, glancing around.

"Yep, everyone loves Hugo's." Wren handed him a glass. He took a slow sip of his wine, clearly savouring it.

"Can we ah, ask about Iris Wainwright?" Jones hesitated, not sure whether she was overstepping the boundaries.

"You can ask," said Christopher, a bit of a grin on his face. "But you know there's not much I can say."

"It's just," Jones looked at Christopher, not wanting to sound like another town gossip, but as someone genuinely concerned. "We just heard some news, and I wondered, has this now turned into a proper investigation?"

Christopher took another sip of his wine, pausing for a moment. He looked at Jones, Wren, and then back at Jones, obviously pondering what he could and couldn't say.

"Let's just say, the interviews you mentioned have become an urgent priority."

"Oh, right," said Jones, understanding the implication completely. It did appear that the police were investigating a crime. Two crimes perhaps.

"Now, enough shop talk," said Wren. "I don't usually see you out of uniform. Tell us a bit about yourself, Christopher."

Jones heard Autumn laugh. Trust Wren to take full control of the situation.

He placed his wine glass back on the bar and asked "What would you like to know?"

"Where are you from, why did you come to Lilly Pilly Creek, and are you married?"

"Wren!" Jones scolded. Jones watched Christopher's face, but he didn't appear in any way offended. He appeared amused and to be enjoying himself.

"Naracoorte, for the Sergeant's position, and no," he responded.

"And no girlfriend?" Wren dared to clarify.

"Ok Wren," said Jones. "That's enough!" She felt a little horrified by her friend, who dared to grill a police officer.

"It's ok," said Wren, laughing. "I'm not asking for me! I *have* a girlfriend."

"You do?" asked Jones, surprised at this news.

Wren grinned and winked. Jones and Autumn both laughed, and Christopher was clearly finding Wren entertaining. "But back to Christopher. I'm asking for the greater good. I must have accurate information for when I am questioned about eligible bachelors in Lilly Pilly Creek, which, might I say, is something I'm approached about regularly."

"Wren, you're ridiculous!" said Jones.

"Well, if it is for such a noble cause," Christopher said, joining the fun. "I guess you could describe me as a bachelor. I'm not sure about the eligible part."

"Oh, you're most certainly eligible!" Wren laughed and then picked up the bottle. "Hugo! Could we grab another one!"

In one swift movement, Hugo grabbed another bottle of Tara's wine and walked over to them.

"Is this what you were after?" he asked Wren cheekily.

"Don't you know it," said Wren. "Jones? Christopher?"

Jones pushed her glass over towards the bottle Hugo had brought, but Christopher declined.

"No more for me," he said. "I'm going to have a busy day tomorrow, and need to be ready."

Hugo extended his hand towards Christopher. "Howdy, I'm Hugo. I don't think we've been properly introduced." The pair had previously met, in tense circumstances, after Hugo had disabled Jamie Royce before he could push Jones down the same spiral staircase Autumn had died at the bottom of. Jones realised however that Hugo and Christopher probably hadn't had a normal conversation.

"Christopher," he responded, taking Hugo's hand. Jones realised this made her feel a little uncomfortable, and yet she couldn't pinpoint why. "It's nice to see how busy it is in here. You're doing well?"

Hugo poured their glasses. "I will say tonight is particularly busy. Another mob heading to the ghost tour."

"Ghost tour?" Christopher asked.

"Ghost *mushrooms,*" Jones explained. "Glowing mushrooms."

"Fred Geier's farm on Dohnt Road," explained Hugo. "He's taking tours until Saturday I believe."

"I had no idea glowing mushrooms were a thing," said Christopher.

"Look, I'm sure you can't answer," said Hugo. "But you know everyone is talking about how Charlie Wainwright's been rushed to hospital. Is there anything we should be worrying about?"

Wren and Jones's eyes bulged as they realised Hugo had no qualms asking the question that was on everyone's lips. Autumn hovered as they all waited for Christopher's response.

Christopher shook his head. "You're right, I can't tell you anything. It's still very early and until the hospital confirms things, there is absolutely nothing I can say. Except," he said. "If you want to go on a police hunch, I don't think this is something the wider public needs to be concerned about." Charlie pushed himself off his stool.

"But Jones, if you can get me your notes as soon as possible, I think I need to go through those."

Christopher nodded his goodbyes and made his way out of the bar.

"I'd be a bit worried if I had any sort of connection to the Wainwright family," said Hugo, topping up the ladies' glasses before walking off to serve another customer.

"Me too!" said Jones. "And based on what Christopher said, that's the way he's thinking too. That someone has it out for the family."

"Jones," said Wren. "I think you'd better be careful. Christopher is right. You've got notes on everyone connected to Iris and Charlie. What if they come after you?"

"Jones!" Autumn cried out, suddenly realising how much danger her sister might be in.

Jones shook her head. "I don't think I've got much of importance," she said. "I can't remember anything particularly revelatory. I imagine Christopher is just ticking all his boxes."

"Oh yeh," said Wren. "He's ticking boxes, that's for sure." She spoke sarcastically and had a sly look on her face. Autumn laughed and Jones swatted her friend.

"Don't be so ridiculous!" Jones took a big sip of her wine, smiling and shaking her head. "Back to the topic at hand. Are we all just assuming Charlie has been poisoned too?"

"Absolutely!" Autumn cried out, which startled Jones but she managed to only flinch slightly.

"Yep," said Wren. "Hopefully it's something completely unrelated, but if I took anything from what Christopher said, it was that Iris and Charlie's illnesses are connected."

"That's what I thought too," said Jones. "I'm hoping we're jumping to conclusions. But if it's true, then someone is out to get the Wainwrights." Jones finished her glass of wine and slid off her stool.

"Leaving already?" asked Wren.

"I want to make a start on the notes tonight," said Jones. "If Christopher thinks they're so important, then I want to go over them before I give them to him. You know, just so I'm clear."

"You should make a copy," said Wren. "Do you have a photocopier at The Memory Bank?"

"No actually, I don't think we do."

"Come past my office in the morning and you can use mine," said Wren. "I'm going to go mingle." Wren looked pointedly at Tara and Prue.

"You are?" Jones was very surprised.

"Why not! I might find something out. Prue is always good to keep on top of the gossip, and it seems she's open to my company. She had no hesitation coming up to us, so maybe she's forgotten about our past altercations."

Jones laughed. "Well, I sure wouldn't be doing it, but go for it, Wren. I hope you find out something!"

"Be careful, Jones," said Wren.

Jones glanced back at her friend, seeing the concern on her face. It surprised her but she did her best to shrug it off.

"I'll be fine," she waved and walked outside.

"Trust Wren to plonk herself down at Prue and Tara's table," Autumn laughed as they walked to The Memory Bank.

"I know! Typical Wren," said Jones.

"But seriously," said Autumn. "Be careful. Do not drink or eat anything where you aren't one hundred per cent sure where it came from."

"Even Sybil's coffee?" Jones laughed.

"I'd be careful," said Autumn. " Seriously. Make sure you see her make it from start to finish."

"Sybil wouldn't be poisoning anyone!" Jones was shocked at the suggestion.

"No, not Sybil," said Autumn. "But someone could slip something in. We don't know how they're doing it, so you can't be too careful. And no more lunches at the winery. You do feel ok, don't you?"

"I'm fine Autumn! Aside from possibly having one too many wines. On that note, I think I'll leave the car and walk home."

"Yes," said Autumn. "That's a smart idea. And it's a nice evening. Cool, but at least it's not raining. But be careful!"

Jones waved as Autumn slipped into the Bank. She walked down the street, pulling her cardigan around her. The idea that both Iris and Charlie had been poisoned consumed her thoughts. It seemed obvious that someone was trying to harm them both, if not worse. But why?

Jones walked past The Lilly Pilly Pantry, its black and white umbrellas folded down for the night, empty dog water bowls reflecting the street lamps. Fairy lights were strung from various buildings, adding charm to the empty street.

Jones walked alone, enjoying the quiet. Were Wren and Autumn right? Should she be fearing that whoever was after Iris and Charlie may come after her? Did she know more than she realised?

Her thoughts turned to the surprise appearance of Christopher at the wine bar. Was that why Christopher had come into the bar? Was he trying to find out how much Jones knew? Did he think Jones had more than a passing involvement in the case? After all, she *was* there when Iris collapsed, and she *had* visited Charlie yesterday, the same day *he* had collapsed.

"Oh my goodness," she couldn't help but exclaim aloud. "Am I a suspect?"

Jones walked home as fast as she could. Her instinct was to call Autumn, but that was impossible. What should she do? Should she be concerned that, rather than being friendly as Jones had assumed, Christopher was in fact investigating her? And how would her interview notes be a part of that? Jones realised she needed to get the notes to Christopher as soon as possible so that he wouldn't suspect her of anything untoward. But, at Wren's suggestion, she would most certainly be taking copies first.

CHAPTER 19

Jones had a fitful sleep. Her mind kept attempting to decipher all the clues they had so far, and when she included herself in the mix, she realised there were many ways for her to be connected to the case. In putting together the Memory Box, Jones was literally at the centre of everyone involved. She had spoken to, and taken notes from all of Iris and Drew's friends and family. She had information that others didn't.

As for motive, Jones couldn't come up with anything plausible. She realised that Christopher was no doubt coming up to the same roadblock. Because of course, Jones had nothing to do with it. Yet, she understood Christopher had to investigate every angle. Should she say something to him? No, that would be silly, especially if he hadn't actually added her to his list of suspects. There was no point in encouraging such behaviour.

Jones messaged Wren and asked what time she was getting to the office. She left her house at eight-fifteen, ready to meet Wren at eight-thirty. It meant she wouldn't run late to open The Memory Bank by nine.

"Jones?" asked Wren, ushering Jones into her office. "What is it, what's wrong?"

Jones sighed. She had been hoping to conceal her concern from Wren but obviously, that hadn't worked.

"I'm just worried," said Jones. "I'm worried that I might be a suspect."

"You!" Wren's eyes were wide. "What are you talking about?"

"What if that's why Christopher was at the bar last night? He said it himself, he rarely goes in there. So why last night?"

"You think he was coming to investigate *you*?" Wren, sitting at her desk, was now resting her chin on her hand, narrowing her eyebrows as she recalled the previous evening.

"Why not? He didn't go and speak to anyone else. And I mean, it's obvious, isn't it?"

"It is?"

"Of course," said Jones. "I was there when Iris collapsed, and I went and visited Charlie the same day he collapsed. Plus, I have a lot of knowledge since I've been putting together the Memory Box."

"But why?" said Wren. "Why would anyone think you would want to hurt Iris and Charlie?"

"I think that's the only thing stopping Christopher from questioning me," said Jones. "At least that's the conclusion I came to walking home last night."

"Look Jones," said Wren. "I think you are probably overthinking this. I mean, you didn't have anything to do with this, so we both know it's ridiculous."

Jones shrugged and raised her eyebrows.

"However," Wren continued. "As your lawyer, I would have to advise you to be cautious. Hand over the notes you're holding, but don't say anything more than you have to. Even if you think you're coming across as rude. This may not even be on Sergeant Schmidt's radar, but let's be careful just the same."

"So you do think I've got something to be worried about!" Jones was beginning to feel sick. Wren wasn't being as comforting as she had hoped.

"No, not to worry about. But it would be nice to avoid accidentally saying something that may put the cogs in motion," said Wren. "So, take your copies, and then give your originals to the police. Stay on the front foot."

Wren showed her into a rear office which was set up with a photocopier, and a large table that had piles of files arranged on top. The walls were lined with bookshelves full of legal-looking tomes.

"It goes without saying," said Wren. "Don't look or touch anything. It's all confidential. I trust you, but I do have to say it."

Wren showed Jones how the photocopier worked and left her to it, leaving the door ajar.

Jones avoided the automatic paper feeder, remembering the horror of her notes getting jammed and torn when she would copy things at The Advertiser newspaper offices where she used to work. Instead, she went page by page, to ensure she copied everything. It was tedious, but she didn't want to make a mistake. As she sat there, she heard Wren's phone ring.

"Hello, Wren Caraway speaking," Jones couldn't help but overhear through the open door. She thought of closing it, but then heard Wren say "So they *do* think he was poisoned?" and her ears pricked up.

"I think I should be there," said Wren. "Of course, it will be just routine, they have to question the sister's fiancé and future brother-in-law. It's procedure. But it's also smart to have legal representation."

Jones put two and two together very quickly. She was speaking with Drew. So *he* was her client. Jones wondered if any of the other Andersons were also her client.

"No, I'm not a criminal lawyer. But let's not worry about that yet. If we think you need some expert advice, I have several people I can call on. For now, let's just get you through this interview......ok.......I'll meet you there at ten o'clock......see you then."

Wren poked her head into the photocopying room. "I presume you didn't hear a word of that, and if you did, you have no idea what it was about?" Wren was shaking her head, making it clear Jones should do the same.

"No, not at all," said Jones. "No idea. And of course, if I did, I wouldn't tell a living soul." Jones smiled, mostly to herself about her last comment. But she also appreciated that her friend had more than likely allowed her to overhear that conversation. She knew Jones would file it away, as she worked on discovering who was intent on harming, or killing, the Wainwrights.

"How's it going?" Wren nodded at Jones's pile of papers.

"Almost done," said Jones. "I'll be out of your hair in a moment. Do you think it's going to be long until, you know," Jones inclined her head in an attempt to indicate Wren's phone call. "Until it becomes public knowledge?"

"If I were you, I'd be stopping at Sybil's before you get to work," said Wren. The two of them laughed, and Jones nodded in understanding. If anyone was going to hear news on the grapevine first, it would be Sybil.

Jones put her last page of notes into the copier and pressed the green copy button.

"Oh, by the way, how did your chat with Tara and Prue go?"

"Well, they're both very entertaining, but they know nothing more than we do. At least, they didn't share it with me. Tara did give the impression she was still very hung up on Drew though," said Wren.

"Did she? That is interesting," said Jones.

"But I just can't picture her being so obsessed that she would hurt Iris," said Wren. "I've known her for years, and she is emotional and dramatic at times. But a killer? I just don't think so."

Jones nodded and started pulling together all the papers.

"Thanks, Wren," said Jones. "I really appreciate everything you do for me."

"What are friends for?" Wren smiled. She knew what Jones meant. Not just for the photocopies, allowing her to overhear her conversation, or for being her lawyer without charging her, but also for supporting her from every moment since Autumn's death. Jones knew Wren understood, but she also knew it didn't hurt to remind her how much she appreciated it, now and then.

With her bundle of notes under one arm, Jones left Wren's office and headed, as suggested, directly to Sybil's. It was ten to nine, so she hoped there wasn't a lineup. Fortunately, today Sybil was parked in between Wren's office and The Memory Bank.

"The usual Jones?" Sybil asked, grinding the coffee before Jones had a chance to answer.

"Yes please Sybil," she replied. "And also a bacon and egg panini, if you have any to hand?"

"Absolutely!" Sybil set to work, and Jones was pleased no one else had yet arrived at the van.

"I presume you heard that Charlie Wainwright is in the hospital?" Jones pried.

"Of course!" said Sybil. "It sounds like he's been poisoned too. Can you believe it?"

"Really? Is this your nurse friend again?"

"Well yes, among others," said Sybil. "And do you know who found him?"

Jones was surprised to admit she hadn't even considered this question. "No, who?"

"Harris! Drew's brother."

Jones gasped. She was genuinely surprised. And then suddenly overcome with the obviousness of the situation. Harris had served Iris her last meal. Who's to say he hadn't done the same to Charlie?

"Seriously? He was there?"

"I'm told he was going around to check on Charlie. Drew had asked him to visit, to see if he was ok. Harris pretended he was returning something of Charlie's."

"What was it?"

"I don't know," said Sybil. "Something to do with preserving food I think. Harris was borrowing it for the restaurant so he just used it as an excuse. Or so I'm told. I imagine he needed an excuse. You know what Charlie Wainwright is like. He's not big on unannounced visitors."

"Oh yes, I know," said Jones.

"All I've been told is that Harris was the one to call the ambulance, and was there when they arrived."

Sybil handed Jones her coffee and turned back to the sandwich press, checking on the panini.

"Do you have any thoughts on who might be trying to hurt them?"

Sybil turned to face Jones, pausing with significance. "Hmm, well, there's a lot of talk. But if you're asking what *I* think?"

"I am," said Jones, taking a sip of her coffee.

"I think," said Sybil, leaning closer. "I think the Andersons gain the most from the two of them being out of the way."

"The farm?" said Jones.

"Yes," said Sybil. "That and the fact that Iris wasn't Davina's first choice."

"For Drew?" asked Jones. "Who was her first choice?"

"Tara," said Sybil.

"So, you think Davina wanted to get Iris out of the way so Drew would marry Tara? And Charlie is just collateral damage?"

"I think that two birds with one stone may have been a pretty good break," said Sybil.

Jones wanted to ask her more, but customers had walked up, and she knew it would be too risky to continue the conversation.

"Thanks, Sybil," she called as she took her coffee and panini and headed to The Memory Bank.

From what she knew, Jones wouldn't put it past Davina to sabotage her eldest son's future wedding. But poisoning? Potentially murder? And had she roped Harris into her scheme?

"Autumn!" Jones called after closing the door on her way in. She hoped she would have enough time to talk to her sister before any customers interrupted them.

"I'm here!" Autumn, unusually for her, came flying in from the rear garden. "How nice is the weather this morning! Seems like spring might have finally returned."

"I bet we go straight into summer with the way the weather has been" said Jones. "But I'm not here to talk about the weather." She slung her handbag onto the counter, and this time it was her turn to slide up and sit on top of it.

"What on earth has happened since last night?" Autumn flew over to her sister, hovering directly before her. Today she was wearing a red knitted jumper and red tartan shorts over sheer polka dot tights. She was clearly in a fun mood.

"Where do I start!" Jones threw her head back, eye to the ceiling.

"Surely you just went home to bed?"

"I tried to but I had a revelation on the walk home."

"A revelation?" Autumn raised her eyebrows.

"Yes," said Jones. "I realised that Christopher is more than likely investigating *me* as a suspect."

"You! Don't be ridiculous!" Autumn let out a short burst of laughter, before seeing the earnestness on Jones's face.

"Think about it," Jones insisted. "Why else was he in the bar last night? And who has been at or near both crime scenes? Me! And don't forget I have been collecting information on nearly everyone involved. Aside from a clear motive, I'm a pretty good suspect."

Autumn had now slowly floated up to the ceiling, pondering what Jones had said.

"Is that everything?" Autumn asked.

"What, you think I'm hiding something?"

"No," Autumn laughed. "No I mean, you implied when you came in that you had a lot to tell me. Was that everything?"

"Well, just that I overheard Wren speaking to one of her clients, who I am ninety-nine per cent sure was Drew."

"So that's why she couldn't tell us anything!"

"Exactly," said Jones. "And, it was confirmed on that phone call that Charlie has most certainly been poisoned."

"Wow," said Autumn. "Did Wren know you overheard her?"

"Yes, she knew I was listening," said Jones. "But I can't let on to anyone that I heard this conversation. The good thing is, Sybil also told me that Charlie was poisoned, so if anyone asks, I heard the information from her."

"Got it," said Jones.

"So, aside from you," said Autumn "Who are our prime suspects?"

"Ha ha," said Jones before taking another bite of her panini and sipping her coffee.

"Davina is high on Sybil's list," Jones responded.

"Davina," said Autumn. "Interesting."

"But that's not all," said Jones. "The conversation I overheard, Wren is meeting Drew at the police station today at ten. He's also being questioned."

"Really! *Drew* is being questioned!"

"Yes," said Jones. "And I think *you* need to be there."

CHAPTER 20

Autumn smiled. She knew what this meant. She flicked her head and a moment later she had a scarf around her head and was wearing sunglasses. Her disguise was ready.

"Oh yes Jones," said Autumn. "Absolutely!"

"It's not wrong, is it?" asked Jones. "I mean, it is, isn't it?"

"Quite wrong," said Autumn. "But what is my purpose on this earth if I can't use my abilities? I mean, seriously, why else am I here?"

Jones's mind quickly flashed back to the previous day when Autumn secluded herself away in the secret room. Autumn was right. Why else was she here? It may be wrong, but who was she to say that it wasn't the right thing to do? Having Autumn on the inside could potentially break the case. It had certainly been one of the main reasons her own case was solved.

"I think you'll have to do it, but she's meeting him in an hour," said Jones. "I"m not sure if I'm going to be able to get out of The Bank by then."

Before they could continue planning the front door opened, and in walked Mr Manowski.

"Mr Manowski!" said Jones. "How lovely to see you again."

"Hello Jones," said Mr Manowski.

"How can I help you today?"

"Well, I was wondering if perhaps you could help me with this?" Mr Manowski lifted a weathered brown satchel. "Talking to you, I realise perhaps my home isn't the safest place for all of these documents. All my family's from when we arrived from Poland. Could I perhaps open one of your, what are they called?"

"A lockbox?" asked Jones. "I would be honoured."

Mr Manowski smiled from under his moustache.

"Thank you. Thank you very much."

"Follow me!" Jones took Mr Manowski over to The Memory Bank counter, and the workday began.

Mr Manowski was very excited by the prospect of opening up his lockbox. "I feel so thankful we met," he told Jones. "I've had my parents' documents in a suitcase under my bed ever since they died. It has always worried me, what with the bushfires we have, and what if I didn't have time to grab it."

"Yes," said Jones. "I know what you mean. A lot of people have put their family history documents in a lockbox because they worry about bushfires. We do suggest people scan their documents too though. Have you done this?"

"Oh no," said Mr Manoswki. "I wouldn't have a clue how to do that. Do you know anyone who can do it?"

"Hmm, well, now that I think of it," said Jones, glancing over to Atlas's office. He was yet to arrive, but Jones had noticed all the equipment he had been bringing in. She wondered if one of the devices might be able to help the Bank's clients. "Leave it with me, and I'll get in touch if I think I've found a solution."

"Wonderful," said Mr Manowski. "So, are we all done?"

"Yes," said Jones. "That's everything! I'll lock this away safely for you."

Jones stood and walked Mr Manowski to the door, whilst also glancing around for Autumn.

"I'll have a chat with Atlas today and see if we can digitise your documents for you," said Jones, holding the door open.

"Thank you, Jones," Mr Manowski said. "Have you heard about the young lady? Miss Wainwright?"

"Still the same I'm told," said Jones. "And did you hear her brother was in hospital now too?"

"Deary me!" he said, shaking his head. "The poor family."

"I know," said Jones. "It is very sad."

As Mr Manowski left, Jones quickly walked back into The Memory Bank, looking for Autumn. She didn't call out as two teenagers were pottering around the gel pens, testing the colours with enthusiasm.

"Autumn," Jones hissed as she walked towards the rear of the Bank. She quickly glanced at the clock. It was nine fifty-five.

But she couldn't find Autumn anywhere. It was then she realised Autumn had already made her way to the police station. For some reason this caused Jones to feel particularly anxious. It was the first time Autumn had ventured out without her. At least, the first time Jones was aware of. She found she couldn't sit still, so she wandered through the shop front, straightening journals on display, removing a candle that had burnt to the bottom of the wick, and lighting another. This fragrance was called 'Vintage Bookshop', one of her favourites.

In between her worry about being a possible suspect in the poisoning of both Iris and Charlie and her worry about Autumn losing energy and potentially disappearing forever, Jones found her stomach churning. She knew the only thing to do was to focus on things she could control, actions she could take. The item at the top of the list was finding out who had a vendetta against the Wainwrights so she could clear her name.

Solving Autumn's energy problem was currently beyond her scope. There was so much they didn't know. Perhaps when this latest mystery had been solved, she and Autumn could spend some time testing how Autumn's energy worked, and find out how they could better manage it. She did feel sad that Autumn felt so stuck. Watching Supernatural, a television show she had binged a few years ago, hadn't fully prepared her for the reality of having a real ghost by her side. She had no desire to get rid of her sister's presence, so the knowledge that to get rid of a ghost required burning their bones, at least according to the fictional Winchesters, was of no use to her. She tried to recall if there were any friendly ghosts in Supernatural, but that wasn't the nature of the show. Perhaps she needed to reach out to the fandom. They would know. And yet, as she thought this, she shook her head, recognising how ridiculous all of this was. Supernatural was fiction, a tv show. The idea that she was using this as primary source material showed how little help she and Autumn could expect to find in their own very unique situation.

The teenagers came over to the counter with their selection of Writech gel pens and excitedly made their purchases.

"I love your colour choices," Jones enthused.

"These are our absolute favourite pens," said one of the girls.

"Yes," said the other. "I can't believe we have them in Lilly Pilly

Creek. All the famous people online use these exact pens. It's so cool!"

"I had no idea," said Jones. "I just liked them myself. I love bullet journalling and these are perfect for that."

"Oh you bullet journal too?" the first girl asked.

"Yep," said Jones. "Although I bet you two are much better at all the calligraphy than me. That is not my forte." The girls laughed along with Jones, before thanking her and saying goodbye.

"I'll order in some of the rarer colours!" she called after them, which seemed to please them as they closed the door.

Finally, there was complete silence in The Memory Bank. She couldn't recall a time in the last few months when she was confident she was completely alone. It was an eerie feeling. Eerier than when she knew she was alone with a ghost. All Jones could imagine was a time when Autumn would be gone forever, gone from The Memory Bank and Jones's life. The idea filled her with dread, and she let out a small sob before pulling herself together.

Moving over to the counter, she took out her original notes and the photocopies and began ensuring they were all in order. From one of the large pigeon holes behind her, she took out two manilla envelopes. One for her copies, and one for the originals that she would take to Christopher today.

She realised she felt sad thinking of Christopher. Perhaps his apparent interest in her, at least according to Autumn, was all a front. Perhaps he was investigating her, using his unusual friendliness. Then her thoughts turned to Hugo. Although they hadn't officially gone on a date, or done anything just the two of them, they had seen a lot of each other. Jones knew she wanted to see him more. It just felt like they were both being extra cautious. Their respective businesses were in such proximity, and Jones spent a lot of time at Hugo's Wine Bar. The idea of them dating and then it all falling apart certainly made Jones hesitate to take things further. She hoped that was also the reason Hugo hadn't done anything. Yet. She hoped it was yet. He always seemed pleased when she came into the bar, and she had spent a lot of time sitting at the bar in conversation with him. So far she hadn't come up with a valid reason as to why they wouldn't make a great couple. Perhaps it was time she made the first move. Yet, where would they go? What would they do? During the day Jones was at The Memory Bank. In the afternoon and evening, Hugo was at his bar. When would they ever find time to do something? Another hurdle Jones would have to jump eventually.

Jones took a deep breath, before sliding the documents into their respective envelopes. As she did so, the door to The Memory Bank opened.

Jones was surprised to see who walked through the door. "Tara!"

CHAPTER 21

Tara smiled at Jones, although Jones couldn't help noticing how tired she looked.

"Hi Jones," said Tara. "Thought I would finally pop in." She turned and glanced around the main foyer. "You've done a wonderful job."

"Thanks," said Jones. "Can I help you with anything in particular?"

"I'll just have a look for now," said Tara. Jones left her to wander through the tables filled with journals, books, candles, and other items The Memory Bank was becoming famous for. One of her favourite new items was a selection of "Messages in a Bottle". Beautiful glass bottles that you could insert a note in, as well as selecting mini items or charms to go inside. She saw Tara took a particular interest in this, examining the small drawers from which you could choose items to slide inside a bottle with your note. They weren't meant to be thrown into the ocean, as the authentic message bottles were, but given as gifts and put on display. However, Jones did wonder how many of these "Messages in a Bottle" did end up on the bottom of the ocean, or perhaps even Lilly Pilly Creek.

"This is such a cute idea," said Tara, indicating the bottles.

"I loved it as soon as I saw them," said Jones. "I had to get them for the Bank."

"Really clever," said Tara. "I'm just not sure if it's quite right." Sadness covered Tara's face. Jones saw a tear fall down her cheek.

"Oh, Tara," said Jones. "Are you ok? What can I do?"

"I'm ok," Tara smiled despite her tears. "It's just, it's everything with Drew. I don't know what to do. I don't know how to help. I thought a gift of some sort, but now it seems pointless."

"Yes, it must be a hard time for him."

"Oh it is," said Tara. "The wedding planning was hard enough for him. But now having to postpone and Iris and Charlie in the hospital. He doesn't deserve this. I know how tough he would be finding everything."

"Did you know Iris well?" Jones asked, her private investigator hat firmly back on her head.

"No, not really," said Tara. "Of course, we saw each other a bit, what with the Andersons always coming to the winery. But I didn't speak to her very often. Of course, I knew Drew well. You know we used to be a couple?"

"Yes," said Jones. "I believe I had heard that.

"We were good together," said Tara. "But we went through a rough patch, and at the time I don't think either of us was mature enough to work through it. I always hoped once we'd had a bit of a break we might get back together. Then Iris came along, and that was that."

Jones was surprised Tara was revealing all of this information to her, especially since Iris had just been poisoned. If she was watching a British murder mystery, she would have moved Tara to the top of her list of suspects. Yet, in reality, surely if Tara had poisoned Iris, she wouldn't be here spouting all this information. And why would she poison Charlie? Unless he knew something no one else did? Jones realised she hadn't considered this alternative. Perhaps the person who poisoned Iris wasn't also after Charlie. Perhaps Charlie was just in the wrong place at the wrong time and needed to be silenced.

Jones glanced around, trying to see if Autumn had returned. She needed to speak with her.

"You were wanting to get Drew a gift?" Jones continued.

"Yes," said Tara. "I just want him to know I'm thinking of him. To know I'm here. But nothing seems quite right."

"What about something he can read," suggested Jones. "While he's sitting with Iris at the hospital?"

Tara looked up, appearing almost confused, before nodding. "Yes, that makes sense. I'll take a look."

Jones watched her walk slowly over to the collection of novels by local authors, picking them up one by one before putting them back down. Wanting to appear discreet, Jones moved back behind the counter and pretended to flip through some of the reports Atlas had left for her. Watching Tara, she saw her pick up one final book, stare at the cover, and without even flipping it over to read the blurb, she brought it to the counter.

"This one please," Tara said as she slid it over to Jones.

"Did you want me to wrap it?" Jones asked.

"Yes," said Tara. "That would be lovely. And do you have any cards?"

Jones pointed towards the card stand and wrapped the book whilst Tara made her selection. She watched as Tara used one of the pens available for sale to write on the card. Jones raised her eyebrows a little at this but ignored it. She had to admit, Tara seemed to be out of sorts, almost as though she didn't quite know where she was or what she was doing.

"Your wine is delicious, by the way," said Jones as Tara walked up with the card.

"Isn't it," said Tara. "The vintage you tried last night is one of our best."

"Not to mention the one I tried at lunch," said Jones.

"Oh right, yes, you came for lunch," said Tara. "Well, that was an extra special bottle. It's not even for sale but I was happy to share it with Drew's family."

"That was very kind of you," said Jones.

"I would do anything for Drew," said Tara. "Anything."

Tara smiled sadly, thanked Jones, and made her way out of The Memory Bank.

"Well, that was interesting," thought Jones. She wished Autumn had been there to hear the whole conversation.

So, she was willing to do anything for Drew. But did that mean poison and potentially murder? Jones didn't like to think so, but after hearing Tara's outburst at the winery the other day, perhaps a crime of passion wasn't beyond her.

When Autumn still hadn't returned, Jones began to worry. It was nearly eleven o'clock. Was this too long for Autumn to be out? Could she be struggling with her energy? Jones had no idea what to do and was annoyed she and Autumn hadn't already discussed a plan of attack for such situations. "What were we thinking?"

Fortunately, Atlas arrived to distract her.

"Atlas," said Jones. "I've just had a customer in. Do you know Mr Manowski, the tailor?"

"I've heard of him I think," Atlas replied, as he pulled out his laptop and got it set up on his new office desk.

Jones leaned on his office door as she spoke. "Well, he needs help digitising the records he just added to a new lockbox, and looking at all your gadgets here, I wondered if maybe that was a service you could offer our clients?"

"For sure!" said Atlas. He smiled and excitedly continued. "This over here is a super fast scanner." He pointed to something that looked like an unusual lamp with a black platform at the bottom. "I bought it when I was working on a video game for one of my clients, and we needed some very specific images to work with for the graphics. I don't get much of a chance to use it now, so being able to work on some of the lockboxes would be perfect."

Jones was pleased. There was no doubt there would be a lot of demand for this service, and she hoped it helped Atlas in his business. She had no idea how busy he was, or even what he did exactly, although she had learnt one thing.

"So, you make computer games?" she asked.

"Yes," said Atlas. "That's one of the things we do. But we code all sorts of programs, and lots of artificial intelligence is being incorporated into all types of software, which we work on. So much is changing at the moment. It's pretty exciting."

"The Memory Bank work sounds a bit boring in comparison," Jones laughed.

"Not at all! Especially when it involves someone's family history," said Atlas. "I love it! I find it all so interesting."

Interesting was certainly a word Jones would use to describe Atlas. Every new thing she learned about him, made him even more of an enigma. Yet she was pleased to have someone like him inside The Memory Bank. He added the modern touch they needed.

"Jones!" She spun around to see Autumn had returned.

"Are you ok?" asked Atlas.

Jones silently chided herself. That was much too obvious. "Yes, I just thought I heard someone." She saw Atlas raise his eyebrows a touch, but then he returned to his laptop and started working.

CHAPTER 22

Turning as casually as she could, she made her way towards Autumn, frowning at her. She waved her towards the stacks and Autumn floated ahead.

"Autumn!" Jones hissed. "Atlas noticed that time. You've got to be careful!"

"Sorry, sorry," said Autumn. "It's just I have so much to tell you!"

"You do?" Jones had almost forgotten that Autumn was on an investigative mission. "First, how are you? How are you feeling?"

"I'm fine," said Autumn. "Totally fine. Barely a flutter in my energy."

"Ok, great," said Jones. "Now, tell me what you heard, but please be more self-aware. I don't want to draw any unnecessary attention to myself."

"Christopher and his colleague are quite the interrogators," said Autumn.

"Oh, were they tough on Drew?"

"Yes," said Autumn. "At least I thought so. But Drew held his own, and Wren was amazing. She's good at her job. Made sure Drew didn't say anything that might lead to anything. You should totally have her in the room if Christopher questions you."

"Gosh I hope it doesn't come to that!" said Jones, putting her face into her hands for a moment. "So, what did you hear?"

"Well, the main thing I learnt is that Wren is only Drew and Iris's lawyer. He approached Wren when he and Iris got engaged. They were setting up their own arrangements, to ensure no one in his family could force their hands when it came to the two farms."

"That is interesting," said Jones. "But does it have anything to do with what's happened to Iris and Charlie?"

"I'm not sure," said Autumn. "But, I do know that whatever arrangements they were making, Drew's mother was not happy about it. This is when Wren let him talk for a while. About the relationship between him and his family. It was almost as though she was leading Christopher away from Drew and towards his family. She's pretty clever."

"What did Christopher think of this?"

"He was very interested in Davina," said Autumn.

"I'm not surprised," said Jones, recalling Davina's manner at their lunch.

"I think having Iris sick and potentially unconscious, means Wren and Drew haven't been able to finalise anything, you know, legally, and depending on how long Iris is ill, it may cause some problems for Drew."

"What type of problems?" Jones whispered, worried she may have missed hearing customers come into the Bank.

"I didn't understand all the legal lingo Wren was using when they were waiting to go into the interrogation," said Autumn. "The gist of it was that now Iris was ill, it put Davina and Wattle Farms in a much better position, as it gave them more time to come up with their strategy."

"So Iris being poisoned *has* had a direct benefit for Davina and

Douglas," summarised Jones. "But what about Harris?"

"He wasn't brought up much," said Autumn. "But there was mention that he was fighting to have the family pay out his share of the farm. The problem was, it seems the Andersons don't have the cash available to do that, and it would potentially jeopardise the farm."

"Very interesting," said Jones. "I'm not sure if that moves Harris higher or lower on the suspect list, but it certainly gives us more information than we had. And would explain why he was so cranky with his parents when I last saw him."

"But that's not all!" said Autumn.

"It isn't?" Jones was genuinely surprised. What more could have happened?

"Tara!" said Autumn.

"Oh, did you see her?" asked Jones. "She was just here, buying a gift for Drew." Jones peered out from the stacks to make sure no one had arrived whilst she and Autumn were talking.

"I know," said Autumn. "And I saw her give it to him!"

"You're joking," said Jones. "Do you think she knew he was in town?"

"No," said Autumn. "She literally ran into him when she crossed the road toward's Wren's office. Like crashed into him. I saw her come out as I was following Drew. She barely even looked for cars when she crossed."

"She did seem a bit out of it when she was in here," said Jones. "So, she gave the gift to Drew?"

"Yes," said Autumn. "And then things got a little dramatic. She was almost hysterical, crying and telling Drew that none of this would ever have happened if they hadn't broken up. It was all her fault and there was nothing she could do to fix it."

"You mean, she confessed?" Jones couldn't believe what she was hearing.

"No, not like that," said Autumn. "I mean, I guess you could interpret it that way, but I don't think that's how it was meant. Drew told her to calm down, that it had nothing to do with her, and the best thing she could do was to help his Mum sort out the wedding."

"Was Drew comforting her?" asked Jones. "Or did he seem upset with her?"

"Upset," said Autumn. "And bemused I think. He'd just been interrogated by the police. Tara was the last person he needed to see."

"How did they leave things?"

"Drew told her to get herself together, and that there was nothing he could do right now. His number one focus was Iris," said Autumn. "That just made Tara sob more and Drew left her crying in the street."

"He did?" Jones was surprised. Drew didn't come across as cold-hearted as that. "Maybe he's a tougher character than we anticipated."

"I think it was just very bad timing on Tara's behalf," said Autumn.

"Did you see where she went?"

"I did wait to make sure she was ok," said Autumn. "She got in her car which was parked near the Community Hall, and drove away. I can only hope she got to her next destination in one piece."

Jones shook her head. It was a lot to take in. The Anderson's challenges with the farm, Tara's dramatic display, and she couldn't forget the fact that Drew had an insensitive streak she hadn't considered before. Would they need to move Drew higher up the suspect list?

"Do you think this information puts me in the clear?" said Jones.

"Well of course," said Autumn. "But who knows how Christopher will interpret it?"

"Maybe I need to fill him in on the confrontation between Tara and Drew," said Jones.

"But you weren't there? How are you going to explain that?" asked Autumn.

"With your help of course!"

"My help?"

"You can feed me my lines as I need them," said Jones. Autumn nodded, smiling in understanding.

"That I can do."

CHAPTER 23

"Atlas," Jones asked. "You'll be here for a while if I deliver my notes to the police station?"

"Absolutely," said Atlas, looking up from his laptop. "I'm planning to be here for the rest of the day, so whatever you need."

"I'm hoping it won't take that long," said Jones. "But I guess you never know with the police."

Jones didn't want to admit to Atlas, but she was a little worried that as soon as she set foot in the police station, Christopher may want to question her.

"Take as long as you need," said Atlas. "I'm not working on anything urgent so I'm fine to look after any customers."

"Thanks, Atlas," said Jones. "I'm loving our arrangement already!"

Atlas grinned and waved Jones out of the office. She happily went and picked up her envelopes.

"Perhaps I need a lockbox of my own?" said Jones, quietly to not draw more attention to herself.

"Good idea!" said Autumn. Together they went through the formal process of setting up a lockbox for Jones. "If we're going to do it, we have to do it properly," Autumn had said as she insisted Jones get on the computer and set up a new lockbox entry.

"I must say," said Jones. "This program Atlas has created so that it automatically takes you through all the steps is very helpful."

"Yes," said Autumn. "He is certainly good at what he does."

"Oh look!" said Jones. "Grandma's name."

Autumn peered at the computer. "You mean Grandma still has a lockbox here?"

"It seems so," said Jones. "I bet it contains all their family history."

"We are going to have to go through that soon," said Autumn, and the sisters smiled at each other.

"Yes, but not today," said Jones.

She found the key that the software had allocated to her and went into the room with the lockboxes.

"It's amazing how many lockboxes have been used," said Jones. "At least seventy per cent. I wouldn't know who had most of them!"

"There is a lot," agreed Autumn. "Many of them have been here since before I started here. Some probably before Dad."

"Do you think some of them have been forgotten?" asked Jones, as she placed her envelope into her new lockbox, and returned it securely to its box.

"Quite possibly," said Autumn. "We may need to arrange a stocktake at some point."

"We," said Jones. "If only 'we' could do a stocktake. I can't think of anything worse!" She laughed at Autumn, but the look on her sister's face made her suddenly feel guilty. "Sorry Autumn, sorry. I know you would love to be able to help with the stocktake."

"It's ok Jones," said Autumn. "I'm ok. I'm just feeling a bit sorry for myself at the moment. But I had so much fun in Wren's office today. It helped remind me that even though I can't do most of what I used to do, you know when I was alive, there is a lot I can do that neither of us would have ever dreamed of. I promise I will try and focus on that. I know there's nothing you can do."

"You know I wish I could change everything," said Jones.

"I know Jones," said Autumn. "Now, shall we go and have a chat with Christopher?" She grinned at her sister and raised her eyebrows.

"What?" asked Jones.

"You know what," said Autumn. "I bet Christopher is going to be thrilled to see you walk in."

Jones swatted her away. "I'm pretty sure he has no interest in me except as a potential suspect."

"I wouldn't be so sure of that!"

Autumn floated ahead, and Jones, tucking the envelope with her original notes under her arm, waved goodbye to Atlas.

"Maybe we should stop in for lunch at Hugo's on the way back?" suggested Autumn. Jones couldn't deny she very much liked that idea, but didn't admit as much to Autumn as they made their way towards the police station.

Although the rain appeared to have left for good, the air did still feel damp and cool. Jones and Autumn didn't speak as they walked. Jones wasn't sure if Autumn was trying to conserve energy, but she did enjoy the sounds of their footsteps and the occasional car driving past.

When they walked into the police station, they were surprised to see Christopher at the counter, almost as if he was waiting for Jones. Of course, he wasn't but Jones did wonder if he was anticipating her arrival for any particular reason.

Christopher smiled when he saw it was Jones. "Ah, you've arrived with the interview notes, I presume?"

"Yes," Jones smiled back, attempting to appear relaxed. "They're all there. I haven't done anything with them. I did take a copy, but other than that, you have the originals. I'm not sure you'll find much, but I do hope they help."

"Police work," said Christopher. "Just have to dot all the i's and cross all the t's."

He started filling in a form before pushing it over to Jones to sign. "It's just to acknowledge that you have volunteered this evidence to us, and we ensure we have a record of when it arrived."

"Will I get my notes back?" asked Jones.

"That does all depend on the direction the case takes," said Christopher. "It is possible, but it can take a long time before evidence is released. Is that ok?"

"Yes, I've got my copy, so that's all fine," said Jones. "Is there anything else?"

"That's everything," said Christopher. "Unless there was anything else you wanted to mention?"

Jones had no idea if he was implying that he was expecting her to share certain information. It was Autumn who reminded her about Tara.

"Not really," said Jones. "Although I did overhear a bit of a strange conversation between Tara and Drew. I'm sure it's not relevant, but she was rather emotional."

"Oh yes?" Christopher did indeed seem interested, despite his attempt at displaying his usual unreadable expression.

"Tara was rather upset," said Jones. "But Drew didn't seem to want anything to do with her."

With Autumn's help, Jones briefly explained Tara's visit to The Memory Bank and then added a small white lie explaining how she was popping out to go to the post office when she saw Tara and Drew across the road.

"And you could hear them from that distance?" Christopher asked.

"Well," Jones bluffed. "they weren't exactly trying to be quiet."

Jones continued to share what Autumn had told her, with much prompting in her ear. Christopher was taking notes as she spoke. It was clear he was taking this seriously.

"Thanks, Jones," said Christopher. "I'll take a look into this. There is a chance I may need to get a formal statement from you, at a later date."

Jones nodded. She found it interesting that he hadn't already taken a formal statement from her, considering she was at the scene of Iris's collapse, but she wasn't going to encourage him.

"No problems," she said. "Let me know if you need anything else."

"Well, that was awkward," said Jones as they left the station.

"What was so awkward?" asked Autumn.

"I felt like I was lying to a police officer," said Jones. "I mean I guess I did."

"Not really," said Autumn. "Nothing you said was wrong. But it's not like you could tell him your sister was the one who overheard the conversation."

"I know, I know," said Jones. "But why do I feel so weird? Do you think Christopher noticed anything?"

"To be honest," said Autumn. "I really can't read him. Except for the fact that he has a thing for you."

"He does not!" Jones felt her cheeks go red. "I'm not interested, anyway."

"Because you're interested in someone else?" Autumn asked, a grin on her face.

"Perhaps," said Jones. Her heart thumped a little as she realised it was the first time she had admitted out loud that she quite liked Hugo. Even if she was only admitting it to her invisible sister, saying it helped confirm that it was true. She did like Hugo, and she hoped something would happen between them. She just wasn't sure when, or how.

CHAPTER 24

Jones knew her cheeks must be pink, but she didn't care. Autumn knew Jones was interested in Hugo, even if Jones hadn't been able to admit it to herself until now.

"Sounds like lunch is in order," said Autumn, who was excitedly spinning in front of Jones. Jones knew she could refuse. Knew she probably should go and relieve Atlas, but she couldn't resist. Perhaps it would be a little quieter, despite all the ghost mushroom hunters that had infiltrated Lilly Pilly Creek.

"Let's do it!" The sisters made their way to Hugo's, Autumn taking the opportunity to twirl and dance a little as Jones walked.

Pushing open the door, Jones was pleased to see there were still one or two tables available inside, and a booth seat. She made her way over to the booth, hoping it might be a little more secluded, meaning she could potentially hold something like a conversation with Autumn without being stared at.

"Champagne?" Autumn asked. "Please?"

"At lunchtime!" said Jones. "I don't think so."

Jones was glad that, despite having numerous wait staff wandering around, Hugo had decided to come over and take her order.

"Any word on Iris and Charlie?" he asked.

"No, nothing," she said. "I just can't work out who would do this to them. Have you heard anything?"

Jones knew that as a bartender Hugo often heard interesting pieces of information.

"Nothing of any substance," he said. "A bit of speculating, but no one can imagine anyone going as far as intentionally poisoning poor Iris, let alone Charlie."

Jones shook her head. "I know. It's so strange and so sad."

"You are being careful though?"

Jones's eyes flickered briefly to Autumn sitting across from her, a knowing grin on her sister's face.

"What do you mean?" she asked Hugo.

He smiled at her. "I can't help but notice that you seem to be ah, in the middle of this current situation, shall we say."

"I suppose it does look a bit like that," Jones said. "But I'm fine. It doesn't have anything to do with me.

Hugo raised his eyebrows. "You don't think whoever is doing this may be a little worried you know more than you realise."

Jones glanced sideways and then sighed. "I guess they could think that," she said. "But I know nothing and have no idea what is going on."

"And you don't have an inkling? I mean investigating is your thing."

She laughed. "Nope, no idea!" At least nothing she was going to share in the crowded bar.

"Well, let me know if I can help!" he smiled at her.

"Help with what exactly?" said Jones, although she couldn't help but smile back. After his involvement in bringing Autumn's killer to justice, she realised he knew her a little better than she anticipated.

Perhaps she wasn't hiding her detective inclinations as well as she had hoped.

"Oh, you know, any brawn or brains as required." Hugo shrugged his shoulders, not taking his eyes off her. Jones and Autumn both burst out laughing at this. Jones had mistakenly labelled Hugo the brawn in their last investigation. However, that is exactly what had happened, and it was Hugo's muscle that had saved Jones's life, along with Autumn's ghost powers. Hugo had refused to allow Jones to talk about it like that, however, insisting the police were right behind him and that it was Atlas who was on top of things having called them. Jones couldn't deny it had been a team effort.

"Now, what can I get you?" Hugo didn't bother pulling out a pen and paper to take their order. He was one of those clever people who could keep it all in his head.

Jones went ahead and ordered a crunchy Thai salad and a glass of lemon, lime and bitters.

"Sure thing," he said, giving her a small salute before walking back to the bar. Jones watched him give her order to the kitchen, smiling.

"Oh my gosh," said Autumn. "When are you two going to go on a date already?"

"Shoosh," said Jones, still unable to take the smile off her face.

"At the very least, you really should talk to him about the case," said Autumn. "We both know you're not involved and know nothing, but Hugo's right. The killer doesn't know that."

"There's no killer," Jones said quietly, her chin resting on her hand, fingers strategically covering her mouth. "No one has died. And for all we know it could be a complete accident."

"Yeh, right," said Autumn, rolling her eyes. "How likely is that?"

"Not very likely, I admit," said Jones. "But enough of a possibility for you, and Hugo it seems, to not let your imaginations get away from you." Jones glanced around, making sure no one was staring at her talking to herself.

"Well, Hugo certainly seems concerned about you." Autumn grinned at her and Jones shook her head. But she had to admit, it did seem that way. The idea that he was worried about her made her tingle just a little. It was nice to know that people were looking out for her. It was even better knowing one of those people was Hugo. Jones couldn't help but smile, ignoring Autumn's knowing looks.

"Back to the case at hand," Jones whispered. "While we sit here, and I attempt to appear sane, why don't you start brainstorming ways this could be something other than an accident, and who might be the culprit."

"It seems obvious that the Andersons are involved in some way. Plus, Harris was the one who found Charlie," said Autumn. "But is that too obvious?"

Jones nodded and Autumn continued.

"Then there's Tara," said Autumn. "She certainly has a motive to get Iris out of the way. But then why poison Charlie too? Did he see something or find something?"

"But Charlie never leaves the farm," said Jones.

"Never, or just not often?" asked Autumn. "We're just assuming he stayed on the farm the whole time. But maybe he has been out. Maybe he's gone out with Iris?"

"Perhaps," said Jones. "But we know for a fact he wasn't at the family lunch and isn't that the place we believe Iris was poisoned? He couldn't have *seen* anything to put himself at risk. But maybe he *heard* something?"

"Here we are!" Jones looked up startled. She had been too engrossed in her conversation to notice Hugo bringing her drink to her. What had he heard? What did he think of her?"

"Oh, thanks!" she said with a smile. "Just talking to myself over here," she joked.

"No problems at all," he said. "I presume it's a journalist thing, you know, getting the facts straight in your mind."

Jones shrugged. "Yeh, I suppose it is. Not that I'm working on a story or anything at the moment."

"Of course, you're not," Hugo replied, nodding and then winking at her before walking away.

"If you don't do something soon Jones, I think I'm going to see if *I* can appear to him! Look at him!" Autumn had now turned around and was kneeling on the bench seat, elbows propped on the back, peering at Hugo behind the bar.

"Autumn!" she hissed. "Sit down!"

"What? No one can see me! I can stare at him as much as I like!" Jones shook her head, but she had to agree with her sister. She was going to have to make a move, and soon.

"It has to be the kitchen," Autumn said before spinning back around to face her sister.

"What?" Jones was confused. Why was she talking about Hugo's kitchen?

"The poison must have come from the winery kitchen," said Autumn. "I mean, I can't see someone being able to slip something onto Iris's plate when it was already in front of her. That would be too noticeable. It has to have been put in her meal in the kitchen."

"Yes," said Jones. "It does seem to be the most likely place. But what was used? And who did it?"

"If it was the kitchen, then it could only be Harris or Tara."

"But how would they have ensured the right meal was given to Tara?"

"She must have been the only one to order what she did," said Autumn.

"Or either Harris or Tara was the one that brought the meals out?"

Autumn nodded. "In the middle of a busy lunchtime, it's unlikely it was Harris. Could they possibly be in on it together? But how are we going to find out?"

"And what did they use?" Jones asked.

"It has to be something in the kitchen. Or maybe it's something Tara uses in the winemaking process?" Autumn clapped her hands, realising she could be on to something. "Maybe it wasn't the food, maybe it was the wine!"

Jones put her hands over her mouth, but this time didn't say a word. She was stunned. Autumn was right. Tara was completely in charge of the wine. Plus, she served particular bottles to the Andersons. She could have easily slipped something into Iris's glass.

People's drinks were drugged all the time.

"Your salad," said Hugo.

Jones looked up at him. "Hugo, I'm going to ask you a question, and you can read between the lines, but please, also take it with a grain of salt."

Hugo's eyebrows narrowed, and he nodded. "Ok."

"How easy is it for someone to slip something into someone else's drink?"

Hugo nodded. She knew he understood her thought process. "Very easily," said Hugo. "People used to have liquid in containers that they would pour in. But these days there are capsules, and also tabs, that get dropped in and dissolve instantly. It's almost impossible to spot anyone doing it, even if you suspect them."

Jones nodded, not taking her eyes from Hugo's. He nodded back.

"Let me know if I can help with anything else," he said, before returning to the bar.

"So Tara?" said Autumn. "We think Tara poisoned Iris?" Her eyes were wide.

"I don't think we can rule out others," said Jones. "But yes, it does seem like the most obvious choice. Although I can't work out how she also poisoned Charlie. We'll need to think about that."

"You know what this means," said Autumn.

"What?" said Jones. "What does this mean?"

"I need to investigate the winery."

"You do?" asked Jones. "I think that's a little risky, and what would you even look for? There could be potential poisons all over the place."

"Yes," I know. "But we need to check, in case we find something suspicious in the kitchen, the cellar door or in Tara's office. I'm presuming she has an office."

"Autumn, I don't think this is worth the risk," Jones shook her head. "I can't allow it." She found it hard to sound determined in a whisper.

Autumn glowered at Jones, but Jones wouldn't say another word. She sat and ate her salad in silence. There was no way Autumn could travel as far as the winery. If anything went wrong, Jones would never live with herself. However, if they were the difference between discovering the truth about Iris and Charlie, what then? Not everyone had a ghost at their side, able to travel places no one else could. "But the police can search all of these places," thought Jones. "They probably already have." So what would Autumn do now to help, that no one else could?

"The best thing for you to do is to eavesdrop," said Jones.

"What do you mean?"

"We need to take advantage of your skills,' Jones explained, speaking with her mouth full to hide her chatter. "Not just cover the same ground that the police can. You can walk through walls, you can listen and watch without anyone knowing. That's what we need you to do."

"Just like I did when the police were questioning Drew." Autumn nodded. "And when Tara and Drew ran into each other."

"Exactly," said Jones. "And at the moment, the two most important people to listen to are Tara and Harris."

CHAPTER 25

"If we really are going to do this, we need to be quick," said Jones. "You know what happened last time."

Autumn nodded, twirling in front of her sister who was standing in the rear garden of the Bank, pretending to plan its upgrade.

"Of course," said Autumn. "Your Mini can move can't it?"

"Oh heck yes," said Jones with a grin. "But we have to be safe. So you need to tell me as soon as you feel even the slightest drop in energy. I don't want to lose you before we arrive back at The Memory Bank." Jones stared at her sister, willing her to get the message.

"What time is the dinner rush do you think?" asked Autumn, referring to the Casa Galati restaurant.

"They're open for dinner from six until eight," Jones replied, consulting her phone.

"Ok, I think we get there maybe around seven thirty," said Autumn. "That way things will have quietened down, and hopefully Tara and Harris will be chatting in the kitchen whilst they tidy up."

"But what about me," asked Jones. "Am I just going to sit in my car?"

"I think you'll have to," said Autumn. "Somewhere dark hopefully. Your car is quite conspicuous."

Jones wasn't sure about this plan. Would they even discover anything? It seemed too risky for too little reward. But Autumn was determined, and after her despair the other day, Jones was conscious of not overruling her sister just because she had more power in the situation. Without Jones, Autumn couldn't travel far by herself, so Jones could easily just ignore Autumn's request. Yet she wouldn't do that to her sister. More and more she thought about how hard it must be for Autumn, living a completely different and most unusual life. Jones shook her head, thinking about that word. Life. Autumn didn't have a life. She only had a death, and even if it meant risking losing her forever, Jones wanted to make sure her sister had the best death she could, no matter how little time that was.

Looking up, Jones saw Atlas walking over to the garden door.

"Shh," she said. "Atlas is coming."

Atlas opened the door and came outside. "Gee, this is a nice space."

"It sure is," said Jones. "Wouldn't it be lovely if we could use it more?"

"What are you thinking?" he asked.

"I"m not sure," said Jones. "Maybe a few seating areas, some shade, and lots of plants. What do you think?"

"What about a few little hidden areas," said Atlas. "Almost like a secret garden."

"Oh yes," said Jones. "I like that idea!"

"I have a bit of time on my hands this afternoon," said Atlas. "I wondered if you'd like me to have a go at scanning the documents you mentioned?"

It took a moment for Jones to remember Mr Manowski's lockbox. "Yes! That's a great idea." Jones led the way back inside. Stopping at the counter, Jones retrieved a key from a small safe they kept there before the two went into the lockbox room. Jones placed the key into the slot where Mr Manowski's lockbox was stored. It clicked and the little door popped open. Jones was able to slide the box out before handing it to Atlas.

"It goes without saying Atlas, that we need to be very careful with all of these documents," said Jones. Atlas nodded. "Not only is everything precious, and needs to be kept in the same condition it's in now, but we must ensure confidentiality. Never leave anything out when you're not around, and if you do need to leave your office, can you make sure you put everything back in the box and lock your office door."

"Absolutely," said Atlas. "I'll ensure everything is taken care of and secure." He nodded at Jones before taking the box.

Jones smiled as he walked away. She did appreciate how enthusiastic Atlas was about his work at The Memory Bank. Even though she had Autumn, she knew there was no way she could do everything without Atlas. It was nice to have him based in the Bank now.

"Is there anything else we need to think of before we leave?" asked Autumn when they were alone again.

"I've been thinking that I need to go through my notes again," said Jones. "I can't recall there being anything of interest, but I at least need to take a look at them."

"I suppose it can't hurt," said Autumn. "At least check that off your list."

Jones went and retrieved her lockbox and set herself up at one of the customer tables. She was able to see everyone in the main area of The Memory Bank whilst she reviewed what she had written in her interviews. Autumn hovered behind Jones, reading over her shoulder. For a while, there was nothing of note.

"Look," said Autumn. "It's clearly written that Harris said he never got on with Drew."

"Yes," said Jones. "But it also says that this was when they were children and teenagers and that they had become closer as they have gotten older. That sounds a little familiar, don't you think?"

Jones looked up at her sister, tilting her head.

"I suppose." Autumn shrugged and smiled. "Ok, let's keep reading."

They continued until Jones read out another passage. "Davina notes that Drew was always destined to take over the farm. He had a love of the farm, and the business brains to take it on."

"Interesting," said Autumn. "But nothing very revealing.

"No," said Jones. "I don't think so either. Although it does hint at Harris possibly being jealous of his brother."

"Look there," said Autumn. "Davina talks a lot about her legacy and that Drew is going to carry on all the work she had done. No reference to her husband. And certainly no reference to Iris. Does that imply that she didn't want Iris involved in the Anderson family's property?"

"If we didn't have two people in the hospital, I would have thought we were reading a bit too much into it," said Autumn. "But we have to consider all options. And at the moment, I'd say the person to get the most out of Iris's death would be Davina."

"Really?" said Jones. "You think Davina poisoned Iris?"

"The more I think about it, the more she seems the most likely suspect. I just don't know how she did it."

"Maybe she had help?" said Jones.

"And who would be most likely to help her?"

"Harris? Tara perhaps. She did seem to love Tara. Or maybe-"

"Her husband!" Jones and Autumn said this in unison. Autumn flew around the table to face Jones and they stared at each other.

"I can't believe we haven't thought about Douglas," said Jones. "The man behind the woman. At her beck and call. Davina is the reason Douglas and his family have such a successful business. He'd do anything for her."

"Anything?" asked Autumn. "Even murder?"

"I have no idea," said Jones. "It just seems our suspect list is getting longer!"

"Tell me about it," said Autumn. "So, who do we have now? Harris, Tara, Davina and Douglas. Possibly Drew?"

"And two or more of them could have been working together!"

"Jones!" called Atlas. "Are you ok?"

Jones turned red. She hadn't realised she had been so loud. She'd almost forgotten Atlas was there.

"Sorry Atlas," said Jones. "I forget that I like to talk to myself when I'm working."

"Working?" he asked, moving to lean on his doorway.

"Well, kind of," said Jones. "I was just going through my notes, trying to see if there was anything that might help Christopher work out what had happened to Iris and Charlie."

"Nice save," said Autumn with a grin.

"Oooh," said Atlas. "Have you worked anything out?" He looked at Jones, eager to hear what she had to say.

"Well, where do I start?" Jones had to laugh. "Let's just say, there were several people at Iris's last meal that seem to have had means, motive *and* opportunity."

"You're starting to sound like an Agatha Christie character!" Atlas laughed and Jones smiled at the thought.

"How are you going with Mr Manowski's documents?"

"Very well," said Atlas, turning to lock his door. "But there is quite a lot there. I'm going to have to finish it up tomorrow."

Jones glanced at her watch and was very surprised to see that it was after five.

"Gosh," she said. "I'd better lock up!"

"I'll see you tomorrow!" Atlas headed out the door.

"I think I'd better get home and grab some tea before our stakeout," said Jones, as she went to tidy up the counter and gather her things.

Autumn laughed at this. "Absolutely! Go and top up your energy."

"Speaking of energy," said Jones. "Are you sure you're going to be ok?"

"Of course I am!" said Autumn. "Don't even think about keeping me out of this. You couldn't do it without me."

"I know that," said Jones. "But we don't need to do it *at all* if it's too risky."

"I'll be fine! Meet me back here at seven," said Autumn. "I'll go and soak up as much Bank energy as I can."

"As long as you're sure?" said Jones.

"I'm sure!"

CHAPTER 26

Autumn was waiting at the front when Jones pulled up outside The Memory Bank. Autumn again slid in through the roof, grinning as she did so.

"Having fun?" Jones asked, looking sideways at her sister, smiling.

A few cars joined them on Main Street as they drove through Lilly Pilly Creek. The Friday after-work crowd were making their way to their next venue. It was still very light, the sun staying in the sky longer during daylight savings. Fortunately, the damp weather seemed to have passed, and Jones looked forward to the warmer days of late spring finally arriving.

Jones couldn't help but continually glance at Autumn. She knew nothing would happen this soon after leaving, but she was worried and didn't want to miss any signs this time.

"How does it feel?" asked Jones. "When you start losing energy?"

Autumn didn't respond for a moment, considering Jones's question.

"It's hard to explain," said Autumn. "The best way I can put it is how I imagine it would feel to have your transparency decreased if you were a photo being edited. Except it's not just your appearance that's diminishing, but also your intensity, your mind, your strength. Does that make sense?"

"Yes I think so," said Jones. "Is it a little like when your blood pressure drops? Feeling like you might faint?"

"Maybe," said Autumn. "Although much more drawn out. I don't feel like I might suddenly faint, but it has that feeling. Like your batteries are steadily lowering."

"Interesting," said Jones. She was trying her best to understand, but it was impossible for her to truly know what Autumn was feeling.

Jones slowly pulled into the driveway of Casa Galati and made her way towards the cellar door and restaurant. "I almost feel like turning my headlights off," Jones joked.

"I don't think that's quite necessary!" Autumn replied. "Although we do want to try and find a bit of an inconspicuous location for you to park."

Glancing ahead, they saw a few rows of cars outside the restaurant. It appeared to be a busy evening. Jones hoped no one was in for a long night.

"Over there," said Autumn. Jones looked to where Autumn was pointing. There was a large container of some sort, sitting at the rear of the building, possibly a cool room. There were no lights in that area, and no windows, so Jones's car wouldn't easily be seen as the sun was lowering. It would also hopefully be next to the kitchen, making it quicker and easier for Autumn to get in and out.

"That looks good," said Jones. She slowly pulled in before turning off the ignition and the headlights. "Now, you're not going to do anything silly, are you Autumn?"

"Of course not!" Autumn acted affronted by the suggestion.

"Seriously Autumn," said Jones. "I can't go through that again. And neither can you. At the first sign that you're losing energy, you need to get back out here. I don't care what's happening inside."

Autumn turned to her sister, looking her in the eyes. "I promise Jones," she said. "I will be back here as quickly as I can." Jones nodded, a slight smile on her face in an attempt to dispel some of the worry she felt.

"Good luck!"

Autumn floated out the roof of the car and Jones watched as she disappeared through the stone wall in front of her.

It was very quiet in the car. The sun was still shining, although low in the sky and Jones did feel a little conspicuous. Fortunately, it seemed unlikely anyone would walk past in the position she was parked. Attempting to control her breathing, Jones did her best not to worry about Autumn. She was confident Autumn would make her way back at any sign she was losing energy. All Jones could hope for was they made it back to The Memory Bank with time to spare. There was nothing she could do now, and she had to remind herself that Autumn had insisted on coming. It wasn't like Jones could shut her out of the car. It was impossible.

Her thoughts turned to Iris and Charlie. The two of them in the hospital, clearly with one or more people out to get them. But who could it be? Jones found herself constantly switching between possible suspects. Davina seemed very keen to have Iris out of the picture, but of course, she wouldn't do the dirty work herself. Harris appeared to have the means and opportunity to carry out the poisoning. But would he be inclined to carry out his mother's wishes? Jones was doubtful. Maybe there was something else between Harris and Iris they didn't know about? Then there was Tara. The scorned ex-girlfriend was always an obvious choice, and she did still have strong feelings for Drew.

It was Charlie that was hard to fit into the puzzle. The only conclusion Jones could draw was that Charlie had somehow worked out who was responsible, and the perpetrator had come back to eliminate him to ensure their secret wasn't revealed.

Jones shook her head. It was all so sad and unnecessary. Why let such things get to a point where the only way out was to inflict pain on other people? She had been through it herself, the pain it feels when someone else has taken the life of a loved one into their own hands. She would never, ever forgive Jamie Royce for pushing Autumn down The Memory Bank spiral staircase. To think she had allowed herself to get so close to him after Autumn's death. The more she thought of it the more anger and hatred she felt. Jones shook her head attempting to force the thoughts out of her mind.

"Well, that was boring," said Autumn, sliding into the car.

"You're back already?" asked Jones. "Are you ok?"

"I'm fine!" said Autumn. "I'll go back in in a minute. There just isn't much to tell at this point. Tara is still out on the floor schmoozing, and Harris is in the kitchen packaging up food. I think it was dehydrated vegetables of some sort."

"Dehydrated food?" asked Jones. "You mean, like the dehydrated food Charlie makes?"

"Oh yeh!" said Autumn. "That is weird."

"Is it possible to poison someone with dehydrated food?"

"I have no idea," said Autumn. "Perhaps if they soak it in some sort of poison?"

"I think we need to research this some more. Unlikely, but we can't overlook a coincidence," said Jones. "Anything else?"

"No, nothing. Harris was just talking about going to the last ghost mushroom tour tomorrow night. Why is everyone so obsessed with them?"

"Oh, I think it would be cool to see them!" said Jones. "Actually, I might join Harris on the tour. Maybe I could get him talking while I'm there?"

"Yes," said Autumn. "Good idea. Ok, I should go back in."

Autumn floated through the car door and returned to the kitchen. Almost instantly she had whizzed back into the car.

"Shh! Put your window down," Autumn hissed.

Jones went to speak but Autumn shook her head. "Don't say a word. Listen. It's Tara and Harris and they don't sound happy."

Jones pressed the button to her window and did her best to hear what they were saying.

"I'm going to get closer," and with that Autumn was gone.

"You've dropped the ball too many times," Jones heard Tara say.

"Seriously, give me some slack! My future sister-in-law and her brother have been poisoned! *My* brother is beside himself. Of course, I'm not going to be thinking straight."

"Honestly, this whole thing has been blown out of proportion," said Tara. "Iris and Charlie have obviously been accidentally poisoned by something in their own home. Honestly, it sounds stupid, and Drew deserves so much better."

"Deserves so much better? What, you mean you?"

"You know what I mean," said Tara. "Not that you treat your brother very well either."

"Why should I treat him well!" said Harris, his voice rising. "He and Mum have been pushing me out of the farm for years. Mum wants to control everything and Drew is her puppet. They don't care about anyone else. It's a good thing Iris-"

"Quick, we need to leave," said Autumn, returning to the car.

Jones turned to her and gasped. She could barely see her sister.

"Oh my goodness Autumn," said Jones. She quickly turned the ignition on, and without thinking, reversed across the gravel, feeling the tyres slip a little as she did so. Ramming the gear stick into drive, she flattened the pedal. For a few seconds, it felt as though the car couldn't get a grip before it shot across the car park. The Mini flew away from the winery.

CHAPTER 27

"Autumn, are you ok?" Jones's heart was racing and she was desperately trying to think of something she could do. The only thing was to get back to The Memory Bank as quickly as possible.

"Can't talk, saving energy," Autumn breathed.

Jones had never heard her like this. Every time she glanced at Autumn she seemed to be fading even more. As she raced the Mini through the dirt roads the sun was setting at exactly the wrong angle for safe driving. Jones did her best to remain sensible and alert but the panic was setting in. Was this the end for Autumn? Had she finally pushed her sister too far?

Frustratingly there was a lineup at the roundabout. "Hurry up, hurry up," said Jones. She would have expected the road to be quieter at this time of night but obviously, everyone else was making the most of their Friday evening. Finally, it was her turn and she accelerated the Mini Cooper into the roundabout, barely breaking as she took the curve, before exiting at speed. The road appeared clear ahead and Jones willed there to be no more delays as she arrived in Lilly Pilly Creek.

"Nearly there," she said, attempting to soothe Autumn. Or perhaps herself. Glancing across, Jones gasped. Her sister could still be seen, but only faintly. Yet, Autumn still looked beautiful. Her eyes were closed, her red hair tumbling down her shoulders. It reminded Jones of her sister laying in her casket. Jones felt tears run down her cheeks. She knew she wouldn't make it in time, it was impossible. She had failed her sister. Failed herself.

"Autumn," Jones sobbed. "I'm so sorry. I shouldn't have let you come. These last few months have been the best and worst of my life. But to work with you at The Memory Bank, it has been better than I've ever dreamed. I know how lucky I've been to have you return. I knew it wasn't going to last forever. I just thought we'd have a little longer. If you can, please watch over me. Make sure I do a good job of The Memory Bank. Send me a sign if you're able to."

Jones's throat now felt as though it was closing. She couldn't say another word, only gulp and let the tears fall. She didn't glance again at Autumn, just focused on the road ahead. Ignoring the fifty kilometres an hour sign, she drove as fast as she dared down Main Street, swung the Mini across the road and up onto the footpath outside The Memory Bank.

Jones turned to her sister. "We're here, we're here." She was relieved to discover she could still see the faint outline of Autumn. Jones had no idea how it worked, but she desperately hoped the energy of The Memory Bank, even from this distance, would start to refill her sister. Jones breathed deeply, trying to calm herself as she watched her sister, looking for any sign that Autumn was regaining her strength.

Autumn's eyes remained closed. She wasn't fading any more, although Jones could still barely see her. Pulling tissues from her handbag, she blew her nose and did her best to wipe the drips from her face and neck. She was sure her collar was damp from all her crying. Jones just watched. Watched and waited.

She knew she had been fortunate to have her sister come back to her. But why did this feel almost worse than when Autumn first died? It was as though their connection had become so much stronger since Autumn's death. Jones realised that for the first time in her life, she had had Autumn all to herself. They were both focused on each other, talking, sharing, and working together, not only in The Memory Bank but also, to their surprise, in 'The Eldershaw Sister's Detective Agency'. Jones didn't know how she was going to cope without it all, without her sister. What would she do? Her life had been turned upside down. Losing Autumn for a second time, would she turn it right side up, or was her current life now her right side?

Glancing at her sister, with no change, Jones leant back in her seat and closed her eyes. She wondered what would happen if anyone walked past, questioning why she was so badly parked, sitting alone in her car, but at that moment she didn't care. She just wanted to stay with her sister as long as possible. No matter what, if Autumn was leaving this world for good, Jones wanted to send her off on her journey.

"Jones?"

Jones's eyes shot open.

"Autumn! You're ok?" Jones turned to her sister, shocked to see Autumn's eyes open, facing her.

"I don't know," whispered Autumn. "What happened?"

"You lost your energy," said Jones. "Almost completely. You had your eyes closed. You weren't moving. I can't believe you're talking to me."

"Where are we?"

"Outside The Memory Bank," said Jones. "I parked as close as I could. I'm up on the footpath!" Jones tried to smile, but she was still very worried about Autumn.

"I can feel it," said Autumn, still speaking very quietly. "I can feel the energy."

"You can?" said Jones. "Oh thank goodness." Leaning back into her seat, Jones exhaled loudly. It was almost enough to have her burst into tears again.

"I think I can move now," said Autumn. She lifted her arms, and then slowly, slowly floated above the car seat.

"Don't push it, Autumn," said Jones. "Make sure you soak in enough energy before you move again."

Autumn floated back down and looked at Jones. "What did we find out? At the winery?"

Jones smiled, feeling like her sister might truly be ok.

"Not much," said Jones. "Except that Harris had dehydrated food like Charlie."

"Oh yes," said Autumn. "That's right. Do we think he got it from Charlie?"

"I have no idea," said Jones. "Maybe. Maybe Harris poisoned it, and then used it to poison both Iris and Charlie?"

"It does make sense," said Autumn.

"But remember we heard Harris and Tara arguing," said Jones.

"Oh yes, that's right. What did they say?"

"They were arguing about Drew, and Harris was going on about his Mum and the farm," said Jones. "The way Harris was talking, he did give a good impression that he had nothing to do with poisoning Iris and Charlie."

"He did?" asked Autumn.

"That's how I took it, at least from where I was. You got closer. Can you remember anything?"

"Just that Tara said something like Iris didn't deserve Drew," said Autumn. "Is that right?"

"Yep!" said Jones. "She sure did. But then you came back when you lost your energy and we didn't hear anything else."

"Oh, I'm so sorry," said Autumn. "I've messed everything up."

"What do you mean? Of course, you haven't!"

"I have," said Autumn. "If you didn't have to race me back to The Memory Bank, you might have heard more of what they were saying. You didn't need me at all!"

"But you saw the dehydrated food," said Jones. "I don't know quite how it fits, but I am sure it is a huge clue. I never would have known that without you."

"If I wasn't there, you would have heard everything Harris and Tara were saying. I bet they would have revealed something, possibly something incriminating."

"You can't know that," said Jones. "Autumn, it's ok. There is nothing more important than having you back. How are you feeling now?"

Autumn lifted her hands, turning them over in front of her. Jones was thrilled to see that her sister's colour had almost completely returned.

"Much better," said Autumn. "Still not great, but I can feel myself getting stronger."

"Shall we get you inside?" Jones unclicked her seatbelt, ready to get out of the car.

"I'm ok Jones," said Autumn. "Stay here. Watch me slip back in, and you'll know I'm ok. You go home and get some rest. You can check on me in the morning. I'm sure I'll be as strong as ever!"

Jones wanted to argue, but she realised there was absolutely nothing she could do to help Autumn. She couldn't even hold her hand. Jones smiled sadly at her sister. "Are you sure you're going to be ok?"

"Jones," said Autumn. "If it's anything like last time, I just need to get inside The Memory Bank and recharge. I'll be ok. I promise."

"You'd better be right," said Jones.

Autumn winked at her and then slowly glided out through the door of the car. She moved around to Jones's side and waved through the window as she floated backwards through The Memory Bank wall, and away.

CHAPTER 28

Normally Jones wouldn't have been able to sleep, worrying about Autumn, but as she drove home the previous night, she came to a revelation of sorts. She had absolutely no idea when, where or how Autumn would disappear. Neither of them had any real idea as to why Autumn returned, or why she was still here. So why did Jones think she had any real understanding of or control over Autumn's departure? And who was to say that it was possible for Autumn to completely disappear if she lost too much energy? Neither of them knew that for a fact. They knew nothing about Autumn's ghost form for a fact. Worrying and feeling guilty was useless and time-wasting. That's not to say Jones still didn't feel guilty, or worried, but she realised that letting those feelings take over things like sleep, work, or solving the poisoning mystery, wasn't going to help anyone, especially Autumn.

Jones still rose early that morning. She decided to take the morning slow, savour the time, and the fact the sunshine did seem to have returned. Last night she had messaged Atlas, giving him the morning off. There was no point having him take the Saturday shift when Jones was going to ensure she checked on Autumn as soon as possible.

Today she chose a t-shirt that read *'It isn't what we say or think that defines us, but what we do.'* It was a Jane Austen quote from Sense and Sensibility and Jones wondered if she should consider it a judgement or an instruction.

It would have been a nice day to walk to The Memory Bank, but after yesterday, Jones felt she needed to have her car quickly available, whatever may happen today. Jones wondered what the afternoon would bring as it was Saturday, and the shop was only open until lunchtime. The idea of curling up in bed with a good book sounded very appealing, but she knew Autumn wouldn't be able to come with her.

"I really need to set up a reading nook at The Bank," Jones thought to herself as she brushed her hair in the bathroom mirror. Staring at herself for a moment, Jones pondered the quote on her t-shirt and wondered what exactly she was supposed to do. Should she pursue the mystery of Iris and Charlie's poisoning? Or just leave it to the police? As yet they had no idea if the information Autumn had managed to retrieve from the winery kitchen was anything of importance. Jones could just pass this information on to Christopher, but then how would she explain where the knowledge had come from? With the possibility of her remaining on the suspect list, Jones realised this was potentially a dangerous move.

Jones brushed her teeth, washed her face, and then massaged moisturiser onto her skin. She applied mascara and blush and thought that would do for today. Staring back at her was a face Jones realised she didn't know very well. At least, not the new version. For so many years she had been Jones Eldershaw the journalist, with a 'very bright future ahead of her'. Now Jones had no idea who this person was or the direction she was headed. Never before had she been without a path nor allowed external forces to move her so far from it.

She wasn't sad, regretful, or concerned. Yet, she was

uncomfortable at times, almost feeling as though she was living in the season of Autumn, the season of her sister, and nothing would move forward until it was determined once and for all whether Autumn was staying or leaving. So far Jones had embraced the Autumn season, assuming it wouldn't last much longer, and that she was required to make the most of it. This morning, however, Jones wondered whether that was the truth. What if Autumn was here to stay? What if she wouldn't actually disappear all of a sudden, one way or another? What if Autumn was going to remain by Jones's side until the day she died? The concept caused Jones to freeze, staring at her own blue eyes, stunned by the concept. If that was the case, what did that mean for Jones?

She shook her head. She couldn't think about that today. Especially before she'd even had coffee. It was time to head to Sybil's.

Jones didn't put an order in today. The sunshine meant it was the perfect morning to hang at Sybil's van for a while and chat. Perhaps Sybil had information that would be useful, for the investigation or otherwise.

This morning Sybil had moved around near the cricket oval, and tired-looking parents of the young children in their whites were lined up for coffee. Jones waited patiently, pulling her emerald cardigan tightly around her. Despite the sunshine, it was still a cool Adelaide Hills morning. Jones desperately hoped summer was on its way.

"Jones!" She turned at the voice and was surprised to discover Wren by her side.

"What on earth are you doing here on a Saturday? What about

your famous sleep-ins?"

Wren laughed. "I know, I know! Love will do that to you?"

"Love? Really?"

"I don't know," said Wren. "Infatuation maybe. My girlfriend's daughter plays cricket, so here I am being supportive."

"That is impressive! Where is she?"

"Who, the daughter?"

"The girlfriend!" Jones was looking over Wren's shoulder for the mystery woman.

Wren waved off towards the oval. "Oh, she's over there somewhere helping kids with balls or bats or who knows what. I haven't watched a cricket match since I was dragged to my brothers' games."

"Well, I am very impressed," said Jones. "This seems like some sort of milestone for you." She grinned at her friend, knowing Wren would appreciate the gentle ribbing.

"Funny what impresses you," said Wren. "And how are you going? Any update on the Iris situation?"

Jones found herself opening her mouth, about to blurt out everything about the previous evening, including Autumn's state, before she gulped, suddenly realising her mistake.

"What?" asked Wren. "What's wrong?"

"Nothing," Jones shook her head. "I just had a weird night's sleep. I guess I'm worried that maybe Christopher still has his focus on me."

"On you? Nah, I wouldn't worry about it."

"Is there something you know that you can't tell me?" asked Jones.

"No," she replied. "Nothing like that. I'm just familiar with the system, and I think you'd be pretty low on the list. Especially with the family that's involved. Not that I said that." Wren winked.

"Jones, Wren, what can I get you?"

They were pleased to discover they had reached the front of Sybil's line.

"The usual for me Sybil, a large flat white. And do you have any of your sultana scones?" asked Jones.

"Absolutely!" said Sybil.

"I'll have two macchiato's Sybil," said Wren.

Sybil pulled out three floral takeaway cups and lined them up. As she pressed buttons on her machine to get the coffee flowing, she leaned closer to Wren and Jones.

"I've heard the results should be back today," she whispered.

"The poison results?" asked Jones. Sybil nodded, pouring milk into her silver jug before starting to steam.

"Interesting," said Jones, pausing the conversation whilst the coffee machine fizzed and hissed.

"I wonder if that will make things easier or harder?" she continued as Sybil poured the creamy liquid into her cup, and a dash on the two smaller macchiatos.

"I heard that Iris is still in an induced coma, but that Charlie is improving," Sybil said.

"Really?" said Wren. "Well, I suppose that is good news."

"For Charlie at least," said Jones. She took her coffee and sipped whilst waiting for Wren whose turn it was to swipe her card.

"I just hope they work out who did this to them," said Sybil. "I know a lot of people are worried."

"Worried?" asked Wren. "That it could happen to them?"

"Exactly," said Sybil. "They know it's probably just a squabble between families, but when the police haven't figured it out yet, people talk and panic."

"Yes, well hopefully someone works out what's happened," said Wren, looking sideways at Jones. "The police, or whoever."

Jones looked down at her coffee. Even without being able to share much information with her, Wren obviously knew Jones was investigating things.

"Here you are." Sybil handed Wren her two macchiatos.

"Thanks, Sybil!" Wren said and the pair walked away from the coffee van.

"I hope we hear about the results," said Wren.

"Oh Sybil will find out," said Jones. "Don't you worry about that!"

Wren laughed. "I don't know how she does it."

"That's the power of being Sybil," said Jones, smiling fondly. "Well, I'd better get to The Memory Bank,"

"You're starting early for a Saturday," said Wren.

"Just want to get a few things done," said Jones. And to check on Autumn.

"Have a good morning!"

"Will do," said Jones. "Enjoy the cricket." Wren rolled her eyes but had a big smile on her face. It seemed this girlfriend may be a little bit more serious than Wren was letting on.

Jones raised her coffee cup in farewell and walked towards The Memory Bank. As she sipped her coffee, Jones was surprised to find her phone ringing in her handbag.

"Hello?" Jones knew she should probably ignore the unknown number, but decided to answer anyway.

"Hello. Is this Jones?" a woman's voice asked.

"Yes it is," said Jones.

"This is Laura Wainwright, Iris and Charlie's mum."

"Oh, hello. How are they?" Jones was certainly surprised to hear from the sibling's mum, and her thoughts immediately turned to the worst.

"Charlie seems better, but we're not sure about Iris," she said, sighing. "Jones, I was wondering, could you come and visit us today?"

"Sure," said Jones, a little taken aback. "Is something wrong?"

"No, no," said Laura. "We just wanted to speak to you. You were the last one to see Iris, and you've spoken to so many people when you were pulling together the Memory Book for the wedding. We just thought, well, we just thought it would be nice to chat."

"Of course, of course," she said. "The Memory Bank closes at twelve, so I can come after that. I presume you're at the farmhouse?"

"Yes," said Laura. "That sounds lovely. Thank you. We'll see you then."

Laura ended the call and Jones paused for a moment. "I wonder what that was all about?"

CHAPTER 29

Jones unlocked the door, calling out Autumn's name as soon as she entered.

"I'm here, I'm here!" Autumn called, sounding a lot more lively than she had yesterday.

Flicking the light switches and disarming the alarm, Jones moved into the foyer.

"How are you? Are you ok?" There was Autumn, sitting on the counter as usual. Today she wore blue jeans and a bright red camisole. Jones supposed ghosts didn't feel the cold.

"I'm fine!" said Autumn, raising her arms and levitating for demonstration.

"Really?" Jones peered at her, noticing her colour did seem bright and vivid.

"Totally and completely fine," said Autumn. She spun in front of Jones rising to the ceiling before delivering a final flip in the air.

Jones was amazed. The way she left Autumn the previous night, she was sure her sister simply wouldn't be the same again. Yet here she was, with as much energy as she'd ever had.

"I simply don't understand," Jones said.

"Me either," Autumn laughed. "Being a ghost is extremely confusing."

Jones had to smile at her sister. The idea that the two of them were regularly surprised by the way Autumn's ghost life worked was ridiculous. How on earth were they supposed to know? And there wasn't anyone they could turn to to ask questions. They were just making it up as they went along. The concept of writing a book entitled 'What To Do When Your Sister Turns Into A Ghost' flashed across her mind, and she smiled at the absurdity of the idea.

"Well that is a relief," said Jones. "It would be nice if we had a bit more warning though."

"Yes, it did seem to come on rather quickly last night," said Autumn. "It's almost like a rubber band where you can pull and pull and pull until suddenly it snaps back."

"Does it feel like that?" asked Jones. "Do you feel the tension as you get further and further from The Memory Bank?"

"In the past, I have a little bit," said Autumn. "I think I still do but it isn't as noticeable as it was at the start. Maybe I'm just getting used to the feeling. I need to get better at tuning in to that side of myself."

"Yes," said Jones. "I think you're right. There must be a way of being able to register your energy levels, you know, like a battery indicator on a mobile phone."

"It would certainly be much easier if a red light started flashing when I was running low," Autumn laughed.

Jones smiled at her sister and, taking the last gulp of her coffee, moved behind the counter to place it in the bin. She then perched herself up on a stool and, elbows on the counter, rested her chin in her hands.

"So, remind me," said Autumn. "Do we have any idea who is responsible for poisoning Iris and Charlie?"

"No," said Jones. "Not really. I just can't get my head around it.

Tara seems a likely suspect, as she is obviously still in love with Drew."

"Yes, and rather intense," said Autumn. "She does seem capable of killing in a fit of passion."

"I agree," said Jones. "Davina also seems like she could be involved. Perhaps she has manipulated Harris or Douglas to do her bidding?'

"Or Drew," said Autumn. "I mean, maybe he had second thoughts, or was being pressured by Davina to cancel the wedding. Maybe he couldn't find any other way out?"

"Drew?" said Jones. "I suppose we should still consider him, but I feel like we're just getting further and further from the truth!"

"I do too," said Autumn. "And I've been no help whatsoever."

"Don't say that!" said Jones. "For starters, you heard Tara arguing with Drew. That was a big deal."

"I suppose," said Autumn. "But I let you down last night. Who knows what else we might have found out if I was better at working out my energy levels."

Jones walked over to Autumn, determined to get the message through to her. "Autumn, you have been more of a help to me than you could ever imagine." Autumn lifted her eyes to look at her sister. "You need to understand how important it is to me that you are here, and I wouldn't want to jeopardise that for anyone, especially in the pursuit of solving a crime. It's police work after all. If we can help so be it, but not at the risk of losing you!"

Jones stared at her sister, hoping the message was getting through. The last thing she wanted was for Autumn to push herself too far and that be the cause of her leaving forever.

Autumn nodded. "Yes, ok, I understand," she said. "I just get so frustrated. I feel so useless otherwise."

Jones frowned. "I know you do," she said. "But you're not useless, not at all." Jones stretched out her arms and looked around her. "Without you, I wouldn't be able to do any of this. So please, don't put yourself at risk. I need you."

Autumn smiled at her sister. "Don't worry Jones. I'm not going anywhere."

Jones smiled back and nodded. "Well then, I suppose I'd better get the shop open," Jones walked towards the door before turning back to Autumn. "Oh, did I tell you? I'm visiting Iris and Charlie's parents today?"

"You are?" asked Autumn.

"Yes," said Jones, unlocking the front door and pulling it open. "They asked me to come to the farm to talk to them."

"Why?" Autumn was floating by Jones, following her as she went through the opening routine.

"I'm not sure," Jones shrugged. "I guess they're trying to find answers, just like we are."

Autumn nodded, turning her head to the side as though trying to process this new information.

With the various sporting activities of a Saturday morning, it was a busy time in the shop. Many people took the opportunity to visit The Memory Bank for the first time since its reopening. Jones found herself chatting with a lot of customers and sharing the story of reopening the

Bank. With Atlas not in that morning, Jones was rather busy. She didn't have the chance to see what Autumn was doing whilst she was serving customers. Jones hoped she was inside the escape room, resting, and restoring her energy to full levels.

Mr Manowski popped in to add some items to his lockbox, and of course, he asked about Iris.

"No change that I've heard of," said Jones. "I believe Charlie may be better. I'm not sure if they were able to treat him more quickly because of Iris?"

"Yes that is probably right," he replied. "Do they know what it is yet? The poison?"

"I think they may find out today," said Jones. "Although I don't think I'm supposed to know that."

Mr Manowski smiled, tapping the side of his nose. "It is ok, I won't tell anyone."

After he left, a few people popped in to purchase some of the drawing and art supplies including Gladys and Neha, who couldn't help drilling Jones for information. "I'm sorry ladies, but I don't know anything more than you do." They weren't convinced but still purchased their usual quantity of goods, smiling and chatting as they left.

An older couple purchased a selection of the local history books and memoirs, the wife telling Jones her family were one of the district's first settlers. "I'm hoping I might find them mentioned in one of these," the woman said, patting the stack of books she had placed on the counter.

"Oh I hope so!" said Jones. "Actually that gives me a good excuse to start reading them all. So I can point people in the right direction when they come in asking about their ancestors."

"You should absolutely do that, dear," said the lady, beaming at Jones. "Perhaps I'll need to come back and share my notes with you."

"Yes please," Jones smiled, ringing up the books and placing them in one of The Memory Bank's canvas bags. The couple waved as they left, and Jones was pleased to see it was noon and time to close.

"I'm heading to the Wainwright's now!" Jones called out, surprised Autumn hadn't made an appearance after the last customers had left.

Autumn casually floated out onto the main floor. "Ok, no worries," she said. "It will be interesting to hear what they say."

"I'll pop back in afterwards, let you know if they tell me anything interesting," said Jones. "You rest, look after yourself."

Autumn smiled. "Of course. Stop worrying Jones!"

Jones rolled her eyes and grinned. She couldn't imagine a time when she wouldn't worry about her spectral sister. Jones pulled the front door shut and locked it. Once she was seated in her Mini, she got out her phone and checked the map, just to make sure she remembered the way to Twelve Oaks Farm. Nodding to herself, Jones clicked on her seatbelt, started the car, and just as she was indicating to move off, she saw movement in the corner of her eye.

"Autumn!" Her sister was now sitting next to her, grinning. "What are you doing?"

"Coming with you of course!"

"You can't! Don't be ridiculous."

"Unfortunately there's nothing you can do," said Autumn. "Come on, let's get moving."

"I could simply not drive," said Jones.

"You could," said Autumn. "But then we'd be sitting here all day and that sounds rather boring."

"Autumn, I can't believe you are being so lackadaisical about this! I don't want to lose you. It's too dangerous."

"Jones," said Autumn, turning to face her. "You've already lost me. I only exist as a ghost, and if I am expected to exist like that, then I can't stay locked in the Bank. I have to come with you and do something. Otherwise, I have no idea what this is all for."

Jones looked at her sister in silence. She tried to process what her sister said, rather than let her emotions control her thoughts. Taking a deep breath, she nodded. "Ok," and moved the car into the road.

CHAPTER 30

The pair were silent on their drive to Twelve Oaks Farm. Not uncomfortably so. Just content being in each other's company. It wasn't long until they saw the Wainwright's roadside stall. Jones indicated and turned into the farm's driveway. They took in the blossoming ornamental pears and flowering irises on either side of them. Jones only hoped her conversation with Iris and Charlie's parents would be a positive one.

Laura Wainwright opened the door. She was a short woman with cropped brown hair and glasses. Her eyes appeared sunken, as though she hadn't slept in many days. Her thin mouth turned down although she attempted a smile for Jones.

"Thank you for coming Jones," Laura said. "Come this way. My husband is in the living room." Jones was shown to a small room. It was filled with old, well-loved furniture, and Mr Wainwright was sitting on a long floral sofa that looked out towards large windows and the rear lawn beyond. He was holding a newspaper but not reading. He didn't appear to notice them come into the room.

"Dear," said Laura. "Jones is here."

Mr Wainwright's head shot around, startled by her words.

"Ah yes," he said, standing slowly. "Jones, thank you for coming." He walked towards Jones, his hand extended. "I'm Mick."

Autumn floated around the room, glancing at everything and peering out the window, whilst Jones was ushered to one of the worn, overstuffed armchairs.

"I'd offer you coffee," said Laura, sitting down next to her husband. "But I have no idea how to work Iris's fancy coffee machine, and so far I haven't been able to find any instant."

"That's fine," said Jones. "I don't need anything."

Mick rustled the newspaper, attempting to fold it back to its original state, not looking at Jones. It was feeling more and more like an interview Jones would conduct as a journalist for The Advertiser, rather than an invitation to someone's home. Jones wasn't quite sure what to do next. It wasn't her interview after all.

Autumn caught her eye and pointed to one of the walls, before giving Jones a wave. She was clearly off to investigate. Jones couldn't help wondering if it should be called snooping.

"As Mick said, thank you for coming." Laura smiled at Jones and then looked down at her hands. Mick had moved back to staring out the window. Jones followed his gaze and notice that from this vantage point, she could see a row of oaks edging the far side of the first paddock.

"Are those the trees Twelve Oaks Farm is named after?" Jones asked.

Laura looked at her husband, and when he didn't answer, she went ahead. "Yes, yes they are. I believe Mick's Grandfather planted them. We love them."

"A pleasant spot to sit and look at them," Jones said, indicating the living room.

"Yes, we used to spend a lot of time in here," said Laura.

"But you live in Goolwa now?"

"Yes, well just over the bridge on Hindmarsh Island. We both like it, although I know Mick does miss the farm sometimes. Don't you Mick?"

"What?" said Mick. "Oh, I suppose. Not the work. Glad Iris and Charlie look after all of that now. Means I can go fishing." Mick chuckled, as though he had said that line many times and a laugh was the usual punchline.

"And have you heard how Iris and Charlie are today?"

Jones looked at Laura and saw tears welling in her eyes. "We think Charlie is going to be ok. He woke up last night but wasn't able to say much. I'll go back in and see him after this. But Iris, they still have her in a coma. We don't know when she might wake up." Laura sobbed out the last word. She pick up a tissue and held it up to her nose and mouth. Tears ran down her cheeks. Mick reached out a hand and placed it on his wife's knee.

"I imagine this has all been very tough, and rather confusing," said Jones. "Do you wonder if this is just one big accident?"

"It's all rather strange," said Laura. "We can't imagine who would want to hurt Iris and Charlie. They're lovely kids. Iris is so bubbly and always so willing to help anyone. She's on all the town committees and is always telling me about the things she's doing."

Mick nodded in agreement.

"And Charlie wouldn't hurt a fly," Laura continued. "He's a bit, shall we say, shy, our Charlie. He doesn't speak to many people and doesn't have many friends. He just loves the farm and his cooking and drawing. I can't see why anyone would want to hurt either of them. To me, it seems like there has been some sort of misunderstanding. I just can't work out what or with whom."

"But the police don't have a clue," said Mick, not able to hide his frustration. "I mean you'd think they'd have some sort of lead by now, wouldn't you?"

Jones nodded. She remembered how the police had told her Autumn's death was an accident when in fact they were still investigating. It had turned out they were investigating Jamie Royce for fraud and hadn't considered he might have murdered Autumn, but Jones did feel it would have been nice to know this at any rate. She couldn't help but wonder if Christopher knew more than he was letting on to Laura and Mick.

"I'm not sure," said Jones. "The police do have quite particular ways they go about doing things. But you don't think there could be anyone out to harm them?"

"Not at all," said Laura, and Mick shook his head in support. "We did wonder if you had heard anything, you know, while you were doing all the interviews?"

"Unfortunately no," said Jones. "I've been no help. Of course, I have provided the police with all my interview notes. And they've seen all the items I collected for the memory box. I've given that to Drew's mum for now. Except, for Charlie's drawings, which he asked me to bring to him."

"Yes, that does sound like Charlie," said Laura. "It would have been difficult for him to hand over the drawings in the first place. He will never sell or give away his drawings. They are quite good." This brought out a slight smile on Laura's face. "And you don't recall anyone saying anything that would make sense of this mess?"

"No," said Jones, shaking her head. "I've wracked my brain. Most people shared stories from when Iris and Drew were both young. And a lot about when Iris was sick."

"Exactly," said Laura. "This is just not fair. Iris has gone through enough. And Charlie, to see his sister sick again. He struggled so much during all of Laura's treatment. Charlie was by her side constantly when she was home stuck in bed or on the couch. He did everything for her, and we were all so happy when she finally got better. And the cancer has never come back. Now, poison? It's all so unbelievable to us."

Bang!

They all jumped. A door in the house had suddenly slammed shut. Jones had the horrible feeling that Autumn had something to do with it, but before she could worry too much Autumn flew into the room.

"It's Charlie!" she said. "And he looks upset."

Jones couldn't reveal this to Laura and Mick of course, but Mick had already gotten up to investigate. Before he made it to the living room door, it burst open.

"Charlie!" Laura and Mick both cried out.

Laura stood up and rushed over to her son, attempting a hug which he swatted away. "Charlie, what are you doing home? Are you alright?"

"I'm fine, I'm fine," said Charlie. "I had to get out of there."

"But how?" Mick asked.

"I walked," said Charlie.

"You walked?" Laura said. "Are you serious?"

"Yes," said Charlie. "I just walked out of there and kept walking. Then I spotted old Clancy Tupper and flagged him down. Asked him to give me a lift."

Jones looked at Autumn and they both raised their eyebrows. They'd had some interesting experiences with Clancy. At least it sounded like he was still inclined to do a good deed.

"I'd better ring the hospital!" said Laura.

"Oh leave it, Laura," said Mick. "I'm sure they'll ring soon enough. I'm surprised they haven't already."

"But what do you need?" Laura asked Charlie. "Should you go and lie down?"

"No!" he replied rather loudly. "No, I don't need anything! I've been stuck in that hospital and now I'm home. Leave me alone. I just need to be alone."

Rudely he strode out of the room and they heard his loud footsteps continue down the hallway until another door slammed and the faint sound of footsteps slowly disappeared.

"Now he'll be in that basement for the rest of the day," said Laura, looking sadly at her husband.

Jones glanced at Autumn before saying, "Well, I best leave you to it."

Laura looked up at Jones, almost as though she had forgotten she was there. "Of course," she said moving towards the door. "Thank you for coming."

"It's ok," said Jones. "I can show myself out. Sorry, I haven't been much help."

"Thank you, Jones," said Laura. "It was just nice to talk with you. I'm sure this will all get sorted out one way or another."

Jones nodded at Mick and Laura, before leaving the living room and pulling the door shut.

CHAPTER 31

"I cannot believe Charlie just walked out of the hospital," said Autumn.

"I know!" said Jones. They were driving back into Lilly Pilly Creek, attempting to make sense of Charlie's sudden return. "I can only hope this is a good sign for Iris. Surely if they were able to fix Charlie, they can fix Iris as well?

"I hope so," said Autumn.

"Was there anything interesting at the house?" Jones asked.

"No, not really," said Autumn. "I did go and take a look at Charlie's office this time. He does love drawing!"

"So, it's more of a studio rather than an office then?" said Jones.

"I think it is supposed to be an office," said Autumn. "Lots of filing cabinets, and trays on the desk with farm documents. But he seems to have covered every surface with items to draw."

"What, like still life?"

"Yes. Mostly botanical items. Flowers, seed pods, fungi, branches, insects. All displayed in different ways."

"Interesting," said Jones.

"He is very good," said Autumn. "I saw the ones that he had put into Iris and Drew's memory box, and they are detailed. There was an amazing one of an ant, from all different angles. And another one with all different types of mushrooms that must be from the Hills I think. They'd look great on the wall at The Memory Bank."

"Perhaps we could offer to sell them?" suggested Jones.

"Yes, that's a great idea!"

"But no clues as to who could have gone to the trouble to poison him and his sister?" asked Jones.

"Not that I could see." Autumn shrugged and turned to look out the car window.

"Meanwhile," said Jones. "I"m starving. I wonder if I can make it before Hugo's kitchen closes?"

"Is Hugo's the only place for lunch in Lilly Pilly Creek?"

Jones wanted to ignore Autumn's jibe but couldn't. She smiled and said "Of course not. But it is the *best* place for lunch."

It wasn't long before they pulled up in front of The Memory Bank. "Will you be joining me?" asked Jones, looking at Autumn.

Autumn shook her head. "No, I think I need a bit of time to recharge. But you will come back afterwards?"

"Sure," said Jones. "I think we need to debrief. I'll grab lunch and then head straight back."

Autumn floated away and into The Memory Bank. Jones locked the Mini and made her way into Hugo's Wine Bar. Usually, she would be apprehensive about eating lunch on her own, but she knew she could just sit at the bar and chat with Hugo when he was free.

Yet again the bar was full of Ghost Mushroom Hunters. Most seemed to have finished their lunch and were enjoying a pint of beer or a glass of wine. Jones found a spot at the end of the bar against the wall. It was a good position because it meant she could lean back and look out across the space, or she could turn and have some privacy.

"Lunch time?" asked Hugo as he walked up. He held out a menu that Jones took.

"Yes thanks," said Jones. "I'm hoping the salt and pepper squid is still available."

"Absolutely!" said Hugo. "We got in extra stock. As you can see, we're busy again today."

"Yes, I did notice that," said Jones with a smile.

"Last day of the Ghost Mushroom tours, so we're making the most of it," Hugo explained.

"Oh yes, that's right."

"Have you been out to take a look?" Hugo asked.

"No," said Jones. "I was thinking about it though. I might see how I'm feeling later on."

"I hear it's quite impressive," said Hugo. "Clearly it's popular!"

"So it appears," said Jones, looking out to the full tables of diners.

"Let me go and give the kitchen your order and I'll come back and get you a drink," said Hugo. He smiled, and Jones couldn't help but smile back.

She couldn't deny it, there was something about Hugo. He certainly seemed to be somewhat interested in her, unless he was just superb at customer service. Who knows, maybe he made all the single women feel this way. Jones shook her head slightly, recognising a habit in herself of doubting anything that may be good in her life. It wasn't that she was going to rush into anything, but why couldn't she consider the possibility that Hugo may be interested in her?

Her thoughts came back to Iris, still in the hospital, still unable to speak and tell anyone what had happened to her. Perhaps she wouldn't know the answer, even if she was awake. If Jones was forced to identify the culprit right now, she would have put her money on Davina and Harris. Jones could see Davina in the role of criminal mastermind. For some reason that was a pretty easy thing to visualise. Whether Harris had allowed her to manipulate him into doing the deed, well that was another thing. Harris did seem to have a mind of his own and didn't appear to be easily pushed around. But was poisoning the lengths they would take to stop Iris from having more involvement in the family business than they wanted? Before Autumn's death, and despite all the stories she had reported on, Jones would have thought it very unlikely. Yet, Jamie Royce had easily pushed Autumn down a staircase when he hadn't received the money he felt he was owed, so perhaps the prospect of the family business being taken out of her hands was enough for Davina to put things in motion.

"So, what can I get you to go with your salt and pepper squid?" Hugo asked.

Jones looked up into his crinkling eyes and took a sharp breath. Her reaction surprised her and she stammered an answer. "A, a glass of the Galati red. Please." She looked down at her hands, and then back up at Hugo. He was smiling at her, and she just had to smile back.

"Sure," he said, somewhat quietly, not taking his eyes off her. For a moment they stared at each other, before Hugo flicked his tea towel off his shoulder, and made his way to the wine fridge. If Jones didn't know better, she would have thought Hugo was as nervous as she was.

Sliding the glass of red to her, Hugo leant down on the bar, moving in closer to Jones. Her mind raced until Hugo started speaking. "Have you heard the news? About Iris and Charlie?"

"Ah, I'm not sure." Jones hesitated, before reminding herself that after all he had done for her, she could trust Hugo. "I do know Charlie is home." Jones tilted her head to the side.

"Is he?" Hugo appeared surprised at that news, but then again, how would anyone else know? Jones had only just left the Wainwrights.

Jones nodded. "He checked himself out. I've just come from visiting his parents and he arrived home. No one else knows of course."

"Interesting," Hugo rolled his lower lip, nodding his head. "Well, that's news. But have you heard that they've identified the poison?"

"Really!"

Hugo nodded and leaned in closer. Jones held her breath at the proximity.

"Mushrooms," he said. "Or at least some type of poisonous fungi."

"What!" Jones said this rather loudly and put her hand over her mouth. Hugo's eyes darted out to the room and then back to her.

"Yep," he said. "Kinda strange, wouldn't you think, considering the crowd?"

Jones spun on her stool and cast her gaze over the room of ghost mushroom hunters. The unlikeliness of the coincidence struck Jones as much as it had clearly struck Hugo.

"You don't think," said Jones. "Could one of the mushroom hunters be the culprit? But why?"

"Who knows," shrugged Hugo. "I can't make sense of it, to be honest. Who? And why?"

"I was sure it had to be someone close to both Iris and Charlie. Is there someone connected to the ghost mushrooms that wanted to harm them?"

"Well, Mr Geier's farm is right on the edge of the Wainwright farm, isn't it?"

Jones narrowed her eyes and thought. She wasn't all that familiar with the various farms in the area. Pulling out her phone she brought up a map of Lilly Pilly Creek that named the local farms. Hugo was right, there, next to Geier's Farm was Twelve Oaks Farm. In fact, the row of oaks lined one boundary paddock between the two, the row of oaks Jones had just been looking at from the Wainwright living room.

Pushing her phone towards Hugo, she pointed at the map. Seeing the location, Hugo looked up at Jones, clearly as bemused as she was.

"That can't be a coincidence," said Hugo. "Right?"

"It seems very suspicious to me." They looked at each other, not knowing what to say next. Fortunately, they were saved by the kitchen bell.

"Your lunch is up," he said and moved over to the servery to pluck Jones's squid from the counter.

As he placed it in front of her, with cutlery wrapped in a serviette, he said one more thing. "If I were you, I'd consider checking out the famous ghost mushroom tour after all." With a wink, he walked away to serve his other customers.

Placing a mouthful of the hot, battered squid in her mouth, Jones realised Hugo was right. It seemed she *was* going to be making an appearance at Geier's farm tonight. Would Autumn be ready to join her?

CHAPTER 32

Jones found herself racing through her meal. Although she usually liked to savour the salt and peppery goodness of the squid and would take any excuse to be in the vicinity of Hugo, the new development made Jones anxious to discuss things with Autumn as soon as possible. She wasn't sure if there was anything they would need to plan before the evening's adventure. And at this stage, she was at a complete loss as to who was the poisoner. The list of suspects was now wide open if she was to consider everyone who had been on the ghost mushroom tour over the past week.

"Yet it doesn't make sense that it would just be a random person," said Jones to Autumn once she had returned to The Memory Bank.

"If it is, it makes our job very difficult," said Autumn.

"Our job?" said Jones.

"Yes, the Eldershaw Sisters Detectives," said Autumn, raising her eyebrows with a smile.

"If we were real detectives, then I would be able to come up with a strategy," said Jones. "But I have no idea."

"I think Hugo's the one with the best strategy," said Autumn.

"So you do think I should go on the ghost mushroom tour?"

"Absolutely," said Autumn. "And *I* have to go too."

"It's not that type of ghost tour!" Jones and Autumn laughed.

"You need me to infiltrate the masses, eavesdrop on the conversations."

"Infiltrate. Right. And what am I supposed to do?"

"You need to ask poignant questions about mushroom poisoning."

Jones scoffed. "Won't that be a little bit obvious! And risky!"

"Well, who else knows how Iris and Charlie were poisoned? Did you get the impression from Hugo it was public knowledge?"

"No, not at all," said Jones, recalling how close Hugo had leant in to tell her. "But I forgot to ask how he found out."

"I'd be guessing Sybil had something to do with the communication," said Autumn.

"Yes," said Jones. "You could be right. But I have to say, I'm just as confused as ever."

Jones was sitting behind the counter, spinning on her stool.

"Me too," said Autumn, who had been, somewhat disconcertingly, floating through tables and bookshelves, seemingly oblivious to how much this was disturbing Jones.

"This morning, I was one hundred per cent set on the culprits being some combination of Davina and Harris. Now I am not so sure."

"It still makes sense," said Autumn. "Harris has been on the tour a few times. And wasn't he planning on coming to the last tour? Maybe that's how he did it. Maybe he collected ghost mushrooms. Assuming they are poisonous. Harris could have easily placed poisoned mushrooms in Iris's meal."

"And Charlie?" said Jones. "Are we thinking Harris fed him at some stage too?"

"Maybe he did bring him some food when he came to visit?" Autumn was thinking hard, moving her hand back and forth through a lit candle.

"I wonder if the police found anything? I suppose he could have brought some leftovers from the restaurant."

"Sounds simple enough to me," said Jones, appreciating the logic of the whole scenario.

"What if it was all just Davina?" suggested Autumn, who had now moved to the rear window, looking out over the future Bank garden.

"What do you mean?" Jones asked.

"Well, maybe Harris is just the messenger shall we say. Slipping poisonous mushrooms into a takeaway container she knew was going to Charlie would be easy enough. And I guess she could easily have put them on Iris's meal if she had access to it?"

"Sprinkled it on top do you think? Would that have been enough to cause enough damage?"

"I don't have any idea of the quantities of mushroom required to poison someone," laughed Autumn.

"Me either!" said Jones. "Perhaps that's something we should investigate?"

"Sure, I'll just jump on Google and take a look," said Autumn. She flew over to the computer at the counter and started mock typing *through* the keyboard. "Hmm, I don't think the computer's working."

"Ha, ha," said Jones. She pulled herself and the chair over to the computer, indicating that she wished Autumn to step out of the way. She spun dramatically away, and let Jones log onto Google.

'How many mushrooms do you need to poison someone?' Jones typed, making a mental note to clear the browser history later.

"It says here that poisonous wild mushrooms are found

particularly after heavy rain," said Autumn. "Death caps are one of the world's deadliest mushrooms, most commonly growing under oak trees or similar. It says they look similar to mushrooms that aren't poisonous, and one death cap mushroom is enough to kill an adult."

"Well, that's not much at all," said Jones. "But what about ghost mushrooms? It seems like they're the ones that were used."

Jones started typing again. 'Are ghost mushrooms poisonous?'

Autumn started reading aloud again. "Apparently you can't eat ghost mushrooms as they are poisonous but won't actually kill you. They can give you vomiting and cramps though."

"Hmm, I'm not sure what to think," said Jones. "It does seem unlikely to have caused the dramatic effects we've seen in Iris and Charlie. But I guess we're not experts. It could explain why neither of them have died. Yet."

"True," said Autumn. "But what that means is, it is possible ghost mushrooms were used. If it only takes one death cap mushroom to kill someone, perhaps a normal serving of ghost mushrooms would be more than enough to cause the level of illness Iris and Charlie have experienced. It just seems to be too much of a coincidence that Lilly Pilly Creek is surrounded by Ghost Mushroom Hunters, and Charlie and Iris are poisoned by a fungus."

"As detectives," said Jones with a wry smile. "We most certainly cannot ignore such a coincidence."

"So," said Autumn, raising her eyebrows. "We're going ghost hunting?"

"Ghost *mushroom* hunting," said Jones.

CHAPTER 33

Jones stood in front of the mirror, wondering if the outfit she had chosen was appropriate for a night of ghost mushroom hunting. Or for tracking a criminal. She was wearing jeans, a pair of brown Dublin River boots that came up to her knees, and a thermal long-sleeve top underneath her sea blue hoodie that said *"We can't be lost if we don't know where we're going."* It was a Lorelai Gilmore classic and potentially didn't bode well for a nighttime walk hunting glowing mushrooms in a paddock.

Glancing at her watch Jones saw it was time to leave. She picked up her phone, keys, and a torch she had almost considered not bringing. Fortunately, she had double-checked the information on the ticket she'd booked that afternoon and discovered this was a requirement.

Jones plucked her navy Kathmandu puffer jacket from the rail near the front door, along with a brown knitted beanie that she believe used to be her mother's. These items were tossed on the passenger seat in the Mini, and Jones made her way to pick up Autumn.

Jones had been wondering if there would come a time when Autumn could spend more time at the house. She had only visited a couple of times, and those experiences didn't seem to indicate that Autumn received the same level of charge as she got from being at The Memory Bank. It wasn't the first time she'd considered the idea that there could be more to Autumn's connection to The Memory Bank than just the fact of having spent a lot of time there and her passion for her job. Surely Autumn would have spent equal amounts of time at their home, and wouldn't the love shared in that home be enough to provide Autumn with the energy she needed? As this didn't appear to be the case, Jones had started to wonder if there was something more they didn't yet understand.

"Of course, there's more we don't know," Jones said, laughing out loud. "I mean my dead sister is a ghost!" Jones shook her head as she pulled up in front of The Memory Bank.

She was surprised to see Autumn outside, standing in front of the Bank's large wooden doors. Dressed in black skinny jeans, brown boots, a maroon tweed jacket, and a cap, she looked every bit like a British country heiress. The light from a nearby streetlamp shone at an angle so the beam of light shone directly through Autumn's chest. It was a stunning sight.

Autumn turned her head at the sound of Jones's car and waved. This time she gracefully slid through the side of the car and into the passenger seat.

"Oh sorry!" Jones instinctively moved to grab her jacket and beanie, accidentally putting her hand through Autumn's thigh.

Autumn laughed. "It's fine! Leave them! I can't feel them anyway."

Jones laughed, but still felt awkward, as she always did when she inadvertently put any part of her body directly through her sister.

"You can't feel the seat? So how do you know where to sit?" asked Jones as she drove away.

"I have no idea," said Autumn. "I think it's just because that is how it is. My body knows that when I get in a car I sit in the seat, so it just does it."

Jones shrugged. "Makes sense I guess."

It was a short drive to the Geier's farm, which was closer to Lilly Pilly Creek than the Wainwrights. It made Jones feel less anxious about Autumn joining her. That hadn't stopped her from having a conversation with Autumn about ensuring she alerted Jones as soon as she started feeling low.

"Feeling low," Autumn had said. "Is that what we're calling it? Surely we can come up with something better than that?"

"I'll leave that up to you."

As Jones turned onto a dirt road, she saw up ahead rows of cars and people, all headed to the final ghost mushroom tour.

"I still can't get over how popular this is," said Autumn as they joined the crowd of people walking towards the entrance to the paddock.

"Me either," said Jones. "I have no idea what to expect, but the level of enthusiasm means my bar is set pretty high. Although I can't imagine a bunch of glowing mushrooms is going to impress me much."

"That don't impress me much," sang Autumn, doing her best impersonation of Shania Twain. Jones had to hold in a laugh as she walked close behind the group of people forming a line to have tickets checked.

Jones looked around, trying to spot Harris. Eventually, she managed to put eyes on him and was surprised to see that his father Douglas had joined him. "Look," Jones whispered, indicating to

Autumn with her head.

"Interesting," said Autumn. "Although I guess it's not that surprising that Harris asked his Dad to come with him. Nothing too suspicious in that."

"Yes, that's true," said Jones.

"Oh, I can see Mr Manowski!" said Autumn, rising in the air and hovering to get a better view. "That's nice he came."

"Anyone else you recognise?" asked Jones.

"Nope, I don't think so," said Autumn. "Oh, hang on!"

Jones felt her eyes dart around, trying to spot who Autumn had seen. When she saw who it was her stomach did a flip.

"Hi! Jones!" Hugo was waving, making his way through the group.

"Could it get any more romantic than a midnight walk to find glowing mushrooms," said Autumn, clutching her hands to her chest.

"It's not midnight," hissed Jones under her breath as Hugo managed to make his way to where she stood.

"Thought I'd join the throngs," said Hugo.

"Don't tell me you're here to investigate," Jones teased.

"Like you are?" said Hugo. "Absolutely!" They both laughed.

"If you think he's joining the 'Eldershaw Sister's Detective Agency'," said Autumn. "You've got another thing coming."

Jones did her best to ignore her sister.

"I'm beginning to feel like this might be a waste of time," said Jones. "I can't imagine what we think we're going to see or hear?"

"Well," shrugged Hugo. "At least we'll see the famous glowing mushrooms."

They got to the gate and handed their tickets to an older woman, who was bundled up in what appeared to be every crocheted item she owned. The outfit was finished with a pair of purple gumboots and a fluffy white hat. She took the tickets from Jones and Hugo with a nod and looked to the next person.

A crowd was mingling around a man who was standing on top of a hay bale, a border collie at his side. He looked like someone who wanted to be in The Man from Snowy River. He wore an Akubra on his head and a Driza-Bone oilskin jacket. This must be Mr Geier. He seemed very comfortable with the attention, unlike the crocheted woman who Jones guessed was his wife.

"Welcome to the final night of our ghost mushrooms tours!" His voice boomed over the crowd like a livestock auctioneer. "This is the first time in all my years that I have seen the ghost mushrooms in November, although my Grandfather used to tell stories of it happening. He said it was a sign of a very, very wet year ahead."

The crowd muttered at this, finding the information interesting.

"Now, there are a few rules for the tour tonight," Mr Geier said. "No touching the mushrooms, please be careful and don't get too close. We've had a few incidents in the past of people pushing each other and falling into the mushrooms." The crowd gasped. "If you do happen to touch any mushrooms with your hand, by accident of course," he raised his eyebrows and everyone laughed. "Please ensure you wash your hands."

"Ask why, ask why," Autumn was insisting. Fortunately, Jones was saved from this by another helpful participant calling out the same question.

"Because the ghost mushroom is poisonous," he said.

The crowd started to sound a little panicky at this, but Mr Geier raised his hands, in an attempt to calm them. "It's ok, they can't kill you, especially if you touch them. But they can make you ill, so I suggest you don't take the chance."

The crowd started murmuring and there was a feeling of agitation throughout the group.

"If you follow the rules, and don't get too close, then you have absolutely nothing to worry about!" said Mr Geier. "Now, there are about eleven or twelve groups of mushrooms, and they extend through two rows of pine trees, so, please, spread out, keep walking. There is no need for everyone to crowd around one bunch of mushrooms. We have an hour, so you can take your time and you'll get to see everything, Please follow the paths that are clearly marked, and enjoy your time with the ghost mushrooms!"

The crowd broke out into applause, returning to its original mood of excitement and anticipation. Mr Geier jumped down from the hay bay in a surprisingly agile manner and called out "Follow me!" The border collie followed him, dashing ahead slightly before returning to his master's side.

"To the mushrooms!" Hugo joked, holding out his arm to indicate Jones could go ahead.

They made their way slowly, not feeling the need to be the first to reach the mushrooms. Jones was trying to listen into conversations, but she didn't think she would catch anything. At least they had confirmed that the ghost mushrooms weren't lethal, although Jones wondered if she could catch Mr Geier and ask him what sort of quantities might potentially cause irreversible damage. Would that sound too suspicious?

Jones managed to keep her eye on Harris and his Dad. Harris was pointing in a certain direction. It appeared he was telling his father that they should make their way down the second row of pine trees. Jones recalled that Harris had been on this tour more than once, so perhaps he knew where the best mushrooms were to view. He had a large camera around his neck, so had come prepared to take some professional shots.

"Looks like Harris Anderson is here," said Jones to Hugo. "Should we follow them do you think?"

"Good one," said Autumn.

Harris and Douglas had reached the beginning of the pines and started striding down the furthest row.

"Sounds like a plan," Hugo said. The two of them, with Autumn floating beside Jones, casually moved in their direction. As they separated from the crowd it started to get darker. Following Harris's footsteps, they moved into the pines. Just as Jones was about to flick on her torch she caught her breath.

There in front of them was a stunning display of glowing ghost mushrooms.

CHAPTER 34

Hugo and Jones stood together in silence. Jones realised she had greatly underestimated the beauty of the ghost mushrooms. There, perched on top of a pine stump, was a cluster of ethereal green mushrooms. The smell of the pine, the cool damp air, and the complete darkness around them made Jones feel as though she had stepped into a fairy world.

Autumn hovered on the other side of the stump. Autumn wasn't looking at the mushrooms, but smiling at her sister. Jones glanced up and Autumn winked at her before gliding away through the trees. She had left Jones alone with Hugo.

"Wow," said Jones.

"I know," said Hugo. "I clearly did not understand what this was all about."

"Me either," said Jones. "They're amazing."

"I wonder if I'll be able to take a decent photo on my phone?" said Hugo.

"We have to try," said Jones. The two of them pulled their phones out, and, taking a few steps closer to the mushrooms, crouched down next to each other, trying to find the best angle to take a photograph.

The two snapped in silence. Jones thought she had managed to get a few decent shots. She glanced across to look at Hugo's phone, and at the same time, he turned to smile at her. She wasn't expecting it and to her surprise, found herself suddenly knocked off her haunches, and firmly seated in a bed of pine needles.

"Whoops!" said Hugo. He stood up and reached his hand out to her. Looking up at him she slowly took his hand in hers. Hugo held her hand for a moment, before eventually helping her to a standing position. They smiled at each other for a moment, before Jones broke the silence. "Did you get any good shots?"

Hugo nodded, smiling. "I think so."

"Shall we see if we can find some more," said Jones.

For a moment Jones didn't think Hugo was going to let go of her hand, but he did, and they began to make their way further down the row. It seemed most of the crowd was still in the first row of pines, so there were only a few groups dotted ahead of them.

They managed to see quite a few more mushrooms, all stunning, but none quite as impressive as that very first cluster. Soon they reached the end of the row, and instead of making their way back down the first row, the two of them seemed to decide to turn in the opposite direction and make their way down the fence line, away from the crowd.

"I'm very glad I decided to come tonight," said Hugo.

"Me too," said Jones. "I would have thought it was hard for you to get away on a Saturday night?"

"Usually it is, but after the ghost mushroom crowd left, it was fairly quiet. My team can handle it. I probably could take a bit more time off than I do." He glanced at Jones and then continued looking ahead.

"I don't think we're any closer to working out the poisoning mystery though," said Jones.

"Nope! I suppose we'll have to leave that to the police," Hugo replied.

"Jones! Jones!" It was Autumn, and she sounded frantic. Jones felt her heart start racing. What if Autumn was losing energy and they had to leave? What would she say to Hugo? But that wasn't the problem at all.

"Jones! It's Charlie!" Autumn was floating directly in front of Jones, moving backwards at the same pace Jones and Hugo were walking. Jones kept glancing up and down, trying not to stare directly at her sister. "Charlie is picking mushrooms! And I think they might be death cap mushrooms!"

Jones couldn't help but stop in her tracks. She managed to hold in the "what the hell" she was dying to exclaim, but Hugo was still surprised by her sudden halt.

"Tell him you see a torchlight. It's not far. If you keep walking up to the edge of that tree, you'll see it anyway."

"Are you ok?" asked Hugo.

"Oh, I'm not sure," said Jones. "I thought I saw something over there." She pointed in the direction that Autumn had shown her.

"Shall we take a look?"

"I guess it won't hurt," said Jones.

Autumn had floated ahead and was impatiently waiting for Jones and Hugo to catch up.

"Can you see it?" asked Autumn. "He's over there. But why would Charlie be picking mushrooms?"

"Look," pointed Jones. "I see a torch light."

"Oh yes," said Hugo. "Gee, you have good eyesight. Do you think maybe one of the group has gotten lost?"

"Yes, that's a good one," said Autumn "Go with that."

"Possibly. We should probably help them."

Unsurprisingly Hugo was very willing to come to a lost mushroom hunter's rescue, so the two of them marched ahead, flicking on their torches as they went. It didn't take them long to get to the next fence, the fence that was lined with the Wainwright's oak trees. Charlie didn't seem to notice them, and they managed to get quite close before Hugo called out.

"Are you ok?"

Charlie's head shot up and Hugo's torch beam blinded him for a moment. Charlie flung up his arm in front of his face.

"Charlie?" asked Jones. "Charlie, are you ok?"

"Charlie Wainwright?" asked Hugo, turning to Jones. She nodded. Jones moved her torch beam across Charlie, and onto the basket he was holding. It was full of mushrooms.

"They look just like the mushrooms he was drawing," said Autumn. "But why would he need so many?"

"Charlie," said Jones. "It's Jones Eldershaw. Are you ok?"

"Jones? What are you doing here?" Charlie's voice was gruff.

"We're on the ghost mushroom tour," she said. "We spotted your torchlight and thought someone might be lost."

"Oh, that bloody mushroom tour," he said. "I'm fine. I'm fine. You can go." He turned and walked away.

"Did you see what he had," said Jones to Hugo. "Mushrooms."

"Mushrooms?" said Hugo. "Like the mushrooms you eat."

"I'm not sure," said Jones, glancing up at Autumn. "But I don't think so. And why would you pick field mushrooms in the middle of the night?"

"So you think," Hugo raised his eyebrows. "You think he's picking poisonous mushrooms?"

Jones nodded. "What do we do?"

"I think we have to call the police," said Hugo.

Jones looked up to see Charlie walking off. "I agree. And I think we need to follow Charlie. I can't believe he's the one who poisoned Iris and then himself, but it seems very suspicious."

"Quick," said Hugo. "Let's jump the fence and try and talk to him."

Hugo pushed the top line of fence wire down whilst Jones climbed over before he followed.

"Charlie," called Jones. "Charlie, I wanted to see how you were. You've just gotten out of the hospital. Are you ok?"

"I'm fine! Leave me alone," said Charlie, marching away.

Jones felt some drops of rain start to fall, and wondered if they were making the right decision. But she had to keep going. If Charlie did have something to do with the poisoning of Iris, she had to find out.

"Charlie," said Jones. "What have you got in the basket?"

"Never you mind!"

"Charlie," said Jones, jogging to catch up to him. As she did the rain started to fall heavily. "Charlie, we found out what the poison was. Did you know?"

This caused Charlie to stop in his tracks, but he didn't say a word.

"The poison Charlie, it's a mushroom. A poisonous mushroom," she glanced at his basket, recognising what he was collecting. "Like the death cap mushroom."

Jones sensed Hugo behind her, but he allowed her to walk slowly ahead. Autumn was floating opposite them all.

"Charlie," said Jones. "Is that what you've got in the basket?" Slowly Jones walked around Charlie to stand in front of him. He didn't look up, keeping his eyes on the ground. Hugo walked further to the side, slightly away from Charlie, letting Jones talk to him.

"Charlie, was it you? Was it you that poisoned Iris? Why? Why would you do that? And then poison yourself? Or was it an accident?"

"I would never harm Iris! Never!" Charlie looked up, his face red with anger.

"But why are you picking the mushrooms now? Why do you have a basket full of death caps?"

Charlie glanced at the basket and then back to the ground.

"Charlie," said Jones. "Was it an accident? Did you accidentally poison Iris? If you did I'm sure the police will understand."

"Understand!" boomed Charlie. "Understand! No one ever understands. They never understand anything. Iris wasn't supposed to leave the farm. She was supposed to stay. Stay with me! And then Drew came and everything changed. Iris didn't want to leave me but he made her. He didn't understand Iris. He didn't understand that Iris and I are meant to stay on the farm together. She wasn't supposed to go with him!"

"You wanted Iris to stay with you?" asked Jones. "You didn't want Iris to marry Drew?"

"I didn't care if she married him," said Charlie. "He was ok. But he wanted her to leave the farm. The house. Our house! She wasn't supposed to leave. She wasn't supposed to leave me all alone on the farm. I can't be alone."

Jones's mind was racing, trying to put all the clues together. Had Charlie poisoned Iris? Or had he been trying to poison Drew and made a mistake?

"But the mushrooms? Who were you trying to poison? Who were you trying to kill?"

"Kill! I wasn't trying to kill anyone!" Charlie looked at Jones with anger before his face changed to a look of devastation. Although hard to see in the rain, tears began pouring down his face. He sobbed, shoulders slumping, dropping the basket to the ground.

"What were you trying to do?"

"I just wanted her to stay," said Charlie. "I just wanted to look after Iris again. I wanted her to remember that she needed me. Needed to stay home."

Jones gasped. "You just wanted to make Iris sick again, like she was when she had leukaemia?"

"Bloody hell," said Autumn. "What was he thinking?"

Looking to her left, Jones saw a glowing light. Hugo had turned on his phone perhaps to record Charlie.

"So how did you do it, Charlie?" asked Jones. "How did you give

Iris the mushrooms?"

"It was just a little bit," said Charlie. "Just a tiny amount in her muesli. She didn't even notice."

"Mushrooms in her muesli?" said Jones.

"The dehydrator!" Autumn cried out. "He dehydrated them!"

"Of course," said Jones, this time replying to Autumn out loud. "You dehydrated them. You dried them, and Iris was none the wiser."

Charlie was sobbing now, his shoulders shaking. Autumn had hit on the answer.

"He drew them, Jones," said Autumn. "He drew the death caps. That's why he wanted his pictures back so urgently."

Jones was shaking her head, it was all making sense. She turned to Hugo. "We need to call the police now."

Hugo nodded and started dialling.

"No!" cried Charlie. "Not the police!" Charlie quickly bent down, grabbed a handful of mushrooms and started running as the rain came down in larger and larger drops.

Autumn flew after him. "He's eating the mushrooms, he's eating them!" she called out.

"Charlie! No!" cried Jones. She started to run after him, but the rain began to pelt down on her face. It was hard to see and she was stumbling over stubble and rock. "Charlie! Stop! Don't do this!"

Charlie ignored her. She could see him putting more pieces of mushroom in his mouth as he ran off in the direction of a scrubby group of trees. Autumn was by his side but unable to do a thing. Jones couldn't keep up and had to let him go. She kept walking, hoping that maybe at some point she would be able to do something.

"Jones!" It was Hugo, calling for her. "Jones, I've called the police. They're coming."

"We'll need an ambulance too!" She turned back towards him, calling through the rain.

"An ambulance?"

"He's eaten the mushrooms!" Jones yelled. "I think he wants to kill himself."

"Oh god," said Hugo. "What is he thinking!" Hugo started running, seeing Charlie racing off in the distance but found the going as tough as Jones. Charlie knew these paddocks better than they did.

"It's too late," said Jones. "Let's just try and keep an eye on him. So we can show the police."

The two of them trudged through the tangle of last year's crop, trying to keep an eye on Charlie and his torchlight, as he drew closer and closer to the group of trees ahead.

Autumn came racing back to Jones. "I'll stay with him, ok," she said. "I'll make sure the police and the ambulance can find him." Jones nodded before Autumn flew off again towards Charlie.

CHAPTER 35

"I can't believe it," puffed Jones as they walked, bracing themselves against the cold rain.

"I know," said Hugo. "He intentionally poisoned his sister to make her sick! Who does that?"

"A very sad, lonely person I think," said Jones. For some reason, although she was utterly shocked, she couldn't bring herself to hate Charlie. Sadly, she understood what it was like to lose a sister, and although she knew she would never have gone to the lengths Charlie had, the idea of losing Autumn again one day could easily overwhelm her if she let it.

The rain poured down and in the distance, Jones could see lightning. A while later the far-off sound of thunder rolled by. She hoped the storm wasn't coming their way.

They came to a small hill and struggled up, nearing their destination, the scrub that Charlie and Autumn had entered. Jones had no idea what the mushrooms would do to Charlie, or how quickly they would work. All she knew was, he had only left hospital that day, and of his own accord. There was no way he was recovered from his first poisoning, who knew what this ingestion would do.

"Do you think that's it?" asked Jones. "Do you think Charlie tried to kill himself but wasn't successful?"

"It looks that way," said Hugo. "And he's trying to get it right this time."

Jones couldn't help but begin to cry. The whole situation was so sad. Scary and sad. She was imagining Autumn there, by Charlie's side, unable to do a thing to help but watch and wait for help to arrive. She was picturing Laura and Mick Wainwright sitting in the farmhouse, likely unaware that Charlie was scrambling around in the rain, potentially taking his last breaths. And there was Iris, still in a coma in hospital, put there by a brother who couldn't bear to be parted from her.

As Hugo and Jones had almost reached the scrub, they heard sirens in the distance. The relief Jones felt almost caused her to stumble. This was the last thing she expected when she and Autumn had set out on their ghost mushroom tour. The idea that Charlie had intentionally poisoned both Iris and himself had never even crossed their minds.

"He's under a tree," said Autumn, who had just flown out of the scrub to meet them. There's a track from behind the cattle yards that leads this way. Tell the police and the ambulance to drive right behind the tractor shed and keep going."

Autumn flew off, and Jones turned to Hugo. "I think we might need to give the police and ambulance directions. Do you want to call them, and tell them to follow the track past the house and behind the cattle yards?"

Hugo narrowed his eyes, clearly confused by what Jones was telling him.

"It's too hard to explain," Jones said. "Just tell them to come. I don't think we'll be able to get Charlie back to the house."

Hugo nodded and dialled, clearly trusting Jones. He directed the police and stayed on the line as they entered the scrub. Even without Autumn waving in the distance, both Jones and Hugo could see the light of Charlie's torch. They ducked under branches and walked around bushes, until they came to find Charlie, slumped at the bottom of a large gum tree. Just as they arrived a huge burst of lighting shone above, and the almost immediate crack of thunder caused Jones and Hugo to cry out. The whole scrub lit up for a moment, and shone brightly on the body of Charlie, still breathing, possibly still conscious, yet with his eyes closed. He had given up.

The sound of sirens wailed close, and Jones could see red and blue lights flashing faintly above the trees. She heard Hugo talking, turning to walk down a track that she could see at the opposite edge of the scrub line. He was directing the emergency services, quietly explaining what was going on. Autumn floated away from Charlie and stopped in front of a storm-beaten wattle tree. Jones walked and stood next to her.

"I can't believe it," said Autumn.

"I know," said Jones, shaking her head. "I never even thought..." She trailed off, unable to say it aloud.

"Not even for a second," said Autumn.

A police car pulled up and out stepped Christopher. Jones was bewildered for a moment, but then felt silly being surprised to see him. She let Hugo speak with him. He had heard everything she had. She didn't need to be the one to explain, this time. Christopher glanced up at her, shook his head, and then walked over to Charlie, bending down and putting fingers to his neck. With Hugo's assistance, they lay Charlie down and got him onto his side. Hugo took off his jacket and laid it under his head. Jones felt the tears return at the sight of this gesture.

"He's a good guy, Hugo," said Autumn. Jones nodded, but couldn't speak.

Finally, the ambulance arrived, and Hugo and Christopher were able to step away, allowing them to take over.

The rain continued to pour, thunder cracking, the sky lit up every few minutes. Hugo stood back, his hands in his pockets, watching the paramedics work on Charlie. They put an oxygen mask on him, shone a light in his eyes, and did various other things, before making moves to put him onto a stretcher. Christopher spoke to them briefly as they loaded Charlie into the ambulance, before he made his way over to Jones, holding a blanket.

"Here," said Christopher. "You're soaked through. This might at least help a little."

Jones smiled slightly and allowed him to wrap the blanket around her shoulders.

"Is he ok?" she asked.

"It's not looking good," said Christopher, shaking his head.

"It was Charlie all along," said Jones.

"So Hugo tells me," said Christopher.

"I couldn't believe what he was saying," Jones said. "Such extreme love that drives you to something like this."

"And mental illness," said Christopher. "Charlie has struggled for many years. Although I don't think anyone expected this."

"His poor parents," said Jones. "Is anyone with them?"

"Yes," said Christopher. "I have an Officer with them now. I'll have to go in and explain what's happened."

Jones couldn't say anything. She was just glad it wouldn't be her having to break the news to Laura and Mick.

"Hugo says he recorded everything Charlie said," said Christopher.

"Yes, I think so," said Jones. "Hopefully it's easy enough to hear. The weather wasn't quite as bad then."

"I will still need to take a statement from you," said Christopher. "But that can wait until later. Shall we get you home?"

"I have my car," said Jones. "But it's over at the Geier's gate. We were doing the ghost mushroom tour."

"That's ok," said Christopher. "I'll drive you around. Then I'll go in and see the Wainwrights."

Jones followed Christopher to his car, settling in the front passenger seat and Hugo joined them in the back. Jones also spotted Autumn slipping in to sit behind her. Before Christopher got in, he took a call. He hung up as he got in the car and said "It's not good news, unfortunately. I'll tell Mr and Mrs Wainwright first but, well, you can guess what the news is."

Jones let out a loud sob. She wasn't surprised to hear that Charlie had passed away, but it was still horrible news just the same. They rode in silence back to the car park. Jones thanked Christopher, and then said goodbye to Hugo, assuring him she was ok to get home, before driving away with Autumn.

CHAPTER 36

The following day, Sunday, Jones slept for virtually the whole day. She had woken, groggily just after three o'clock, very confused as to what time it was, and what had happened. The thoughts all came rushing back to her, and she curled up in a ball, pulling the quilt over her head.

The idea that Charlie was responsible for poisoning not only Iris, but himself, was just too unbelievable. And yet it was true, and now Charlie was dead. She could only hope the same fate wouldn't befall Iris.

Jones remained in her bed for another hour, before she heard the sound of her mobile phone ringing. It took her a moment to discover it, still in the pocket of her jacket, that she had thrown on the floor under the window.

"Hello?"

"Jones, it's Atlas."

"Oh, hi Atlas," said Jones. She knew she must sound very groggy.

"I'm at the pub with Hugo and he's been filling Wren and me in on your adventures last night. Are you ok?"

"Yes," said Jones, leaning back on her bed head, and pulling the covers over her legs. "Yes, I'm fine. Although I have been asleep nearly all day."

"I'm not surprised," said Atlas. "I'm going to put it on speaker phone if that's ok. It's just us. Hugo closed the bar early today."

"Sure, sure," said Jones, wondering why the need for everyone to be on the call.

"Hi Jones," called Wren.

"Hi Jones," said Hugo.

"Hi everyone," said Jones. "But I'm fine. I just needed a bit of sleep."

"We wanted to tell you," said Wren. "To let you know what was happening."

Jones couldn't read her friend's voice, but it didn't sound in too much distress.

"What is it?"

"It's Iris," said Wren. "She's woken up!"

"Oh thank goodness!" said Jones, and she found herself suddenly bursting into tears. The relief she felt was unexpected after the night she had just gone through. "Is she ok?"

"From what we hear, she'll make a full recovery," said Wren.

"They haven't told her about Charlie yet," said Hugo. "Drew popped into the bar just as I was closing to grab a bottle of champagne. He'd gone to visit the Wainwrights and they were all together when they got the news."

"Drew was pretty annoyed with himself for not being there when she woke up," said Atlas. "But he was so happy she was awake. He couldn't stop smiling."

"Oh," said Jones. "That's lovely. But poor Iris, when she hears about Charlie. It will break her heart."

"It will," said Wren. "But she has Drew and her parents. She'll be ok."

"Thanks for letting me know," said Jones. "I'm so pleased."

"Do you need anything?" asked Hugo.

Jones couldn't help but smile, and was glad no one was there to see her. "No thanks, I'm fine. I think I'm going to grab a quick bite to eat and watch some tv in bed." The longer she was awake the more she realised how much her body was aching after the previous evening bounding across the paddocks.

"Look after yourself," said Wren. "I'll give you a call tomorrow."

"What day is it tomorrow?" asked Jones. "Monday, right?"

"Yep," said Atlas. "I can open up The Memory Bank Jones. Maybe you need a day off."

"I think you're right Atlas," said Jones. "Thank you."

They all said goodbye and Jones leant her head back, closing her eyes. After losing their son, thank goodness Laura and Mick had some happy news.

A toasted cheese sandwich and a cup of tea were all Jones could manage for a late lunch. As promised, she curled up in bed with a tv show streaming on her laptop, but it wasn't long before he eyelids grew heavy and, closing the laptop, she fell into another deep sleep.

The next time she woke it was to the sound of singing. As she rolled over in her bed, eyes still closed, she smiled.

"Good morning Autumn," said Jones.

"Good morning Jones," her sister replied. "Do you think you'll make it out of bed today?" Jones opened her eyes to see Autumn grinning.

"What day is it?"

"It's Monday," said Autumn. "Just after eleven."

"Atlas is in charge today," Jones said. "Did you hear the news?"

"It was all anyone could talk about in The Memory Bank this morning," Autumn smiled and Jones smiled back. Knowing Iris was awake and would be ok was the best possible outcome after a traumatic week.

"I've been checking on you," said Autumn. "But every time I visited, your snoring let me know you were ok."

"I don't snore," Jones replied, smiling sheepishly.

"Oh no," said Autumn. "Not at all."

Jones sat up and stretched her arms above her head, letting out a long yawn.

"I see no reason to leave this bed, except for food and the toilet," said Jones. "Want to join me?"

"I couldn't think of anything better!"

SIGN UP TO MY NEWSLETTER

Thank you so much for reading The Bride of Lilly Pilly Creek. If you enjoyed the book and would like to be notified when new books in the Lilly Pilly Creek Ghost Mysteries series are released, or other titles, I would love it if you would sign up to receive my newsletter. Every now and then you may receive exclusive free bonus material, as well as my latest news or when titles go on sale. If you would like to sign up please visit my website abbielmartin.com

ABOUT THE AUTHOR

Abbie L. Martin is a South Australian author who lives with her family in a small town very similar to Lilly Pilly Creek. She has been dreaming of writing and publishing since she was a child, and when she reached her forties, finally decided to take the leap. Whilst also running a business with her husband, and juggling life with three children, Abbie loves nothing better than peace and quiet with a good book and a glass of wine, preferably an Adelaide Hills sparkling.

BY ABBIE L. MARTIN

The Lilly Pilly Creek Ghost Mystery Series

Book 1 - The Ghost of Lilly Pilly Creek

Book 2 - The Bride of Lilly Pilly Creek

Made in the USA
Monee, IL
13 July 2024

61768872R00134